The Secret Kitten
and other tales

The Secret Kitten

and other tales

by Holly Webb

Illustrated by Sophy Williams

tiger tales

tiger tales

5 River Road, Suite 128, Wilton, CT 06897
Published in the United States 2020
Text copyright © Holly Webb
The Secret Kitten 2015
Sammy the Shy Kitten 2016
The Brave Kitten 2016
Illustrations copyright © Sophy Williams
The Secret Kitten 2015
Sammy the Shy Kitten 2016
The Brave Kitten 2016
ISBN-13: 978-1-68010-477-6
ISBN-10: 1-68010-477-2
Printed in the USA
STP/4800/0382/0920
10 9 8 7 6 5 4 3 2

For more insight and activities, visit us at www.tigertalesbooks.com

Contents

The
Secret
Kitten

Contents

For Poppy and Star, my not-so-secret kittens…

Chapter One
A New Beginning

Alicia stood on tiptoe with her elbows balanced on the windowsill, leaning out to look down at the yard. She had never had a room like this before, right up at the very top of the house. She was so high up that the yard looked strange and far below, the trees short and stubby, even though she knew that they were tall.

Actually, she had never had a room of her own before. She had always shared with Will, her little brother. But now that they were living at Grandma's house, there was space for each of them to have their own room. It was nice and really odd at the same time.

Alicia had mixed feelings about everything at the moment. Grandma's house was beautiful with a big yard, not like the tiny yard she'd had back home, but she couldn't stop thinking about the old house. They had been to Grandma's many times, of course, but always as visitors. Living here was going to be strange and different. The house didn't feel like it was their home yet, even though Dad had explained that he'd bought half of it from Grandma. They were all going to share. Grandma would help take care of Alicia and Will, and Dad would take care of the wild, overgrown yard that had gotten to be too much for Grandma recently, and they would all be company for each other.

It will be good for Dad, Alicia thought, resting her chin on her hands as she stared down at the trees. For the last five years, ever since their mom had died, he'd taken care of Will and her by himself. He'd had a little help from babysitters, but mostly he had been in charge of everything. Now he would have Grandma to help and maybe he wouldn't be so worried all the time. It was hard when he had to stay late at work and missed picking up Alicia and Will from after-school clubs, or the babysitter's, or their friends' houses.

Alicia swallowed hard. They wouldn't be going back to their after-school clubs. They weren't even going back to their old school—Grandma's house was too far away. On Monday, she and Will would be starting all over again at a new school.

Alicia wasn't looking forward to it.

"It'll be all right," Alicia whispered to herself. "It was nice when we went to see it." The teacher had been friendly and kind, Will had loved the big jungle gym on the playground, and it was only a five-minute walk from Grandma's house. But it was new and different, and even though there would be a coat hook ready with her name on it and a desk for her books in the classroom, Alicia knew she didn't really belong there, not yet.

Something stirred among the trees. Alicia squinted sideways, trying to figure out what it was. A bird? Then she smiled. A large orange cat was walking carefully along the fence, padding from paw to paw, slowly and deliberately. *He must belong next door*, Alicia thought.

Grandma didn't have a cat. She didn't have any pets, even though this would be the perfect house for one with its beautiful big yard. Alicia thought Grandma's neat living room would look a lot nicer with a cat draped along the back of the sofa, or curled up on the rug.

But Dad had told them that Grandma didn't like pets. She thought they were too messy and were a lot of work. Alicia wished she could argue with Grandma and say what about purring and how a cat could keep your feet warm on a cold night. But you couldn't start that kind of argument with your grandma—not her grandma, anyway. She wasn't an arguing kind of person. Alicia loved her, but Grandma was one of those people who knew she was always right. And she was the one who would be doing most of the cleaning up, too!

"Alicia!"

It was Will! Alicia spun around, hearing the wobbly, tearful note in his voice. "What's the matter?" she asked worriedly.

"Grandma yelled at me," Will sniffed. He sat down on the floor, leaning against Alicia's bed. His face was flushed, and he brushed away a tear with his hand.

"Why?" Alicia sat next to him and put her arm around his shoulders.

Will snuggled into her. "I was playing soccer in the yard and then I brought the ball back in with me and I bounced it...."

"Oh, Will! Where?" Alicia demanded, and he edged away from her a little, hunching his shoulders up.

"In the living room."

"You didn't break anything, did you?" Alicia asked anxiously. Dad had made them promise to be careful, but Will was only six, and sometimes he just forgot things like that.

"No!" Will protested indignantly. "But Grandma was still really angry. She said I wasn't supposed to kick balls around in the house, but I hadn't even kicked it! I was just bouncing it." He sighed and leaned back on her shoulder again, peering around Alicia's room at the cardboard boxes, already almost all unpacked.

"Do you like having your own bedroom?" he whispered seriously.

Alicia nodded. "Yes…. But last night I missed hearing you talking to your toys," she added to make him feel better.

"I do like my bedroom." Will didn't sound so sure. "But do you think I could keep all my things in my room, then sleep up here with you? I could bring my sleeping bag."

"Maybe sometimes," Alicia said comfortingly. It had been strange going to bed last night without Will snoring and snuffling on the other side of the room, but she was glad to have a place that was just her own.

All her own, except that it would be so nice to share it with a cat. *Any cat*, Alicia thought, wondering if the big orange cat from next door ever came to visit.

Chapter Two
Kittens!

The black-and-white kitten peered around the pile of old boxes. Her ears were laid back flat, and her tail was twitching. Out in the alley between the bakery and newsstand, she could see her brother and sister playing around, chasing each other and wrestling. Her paws itched to join in. She stepped out a little farther.

Then a car roared past on the main road, and she darted back into her hiding place in the storage yard. Seconds later, her tabby brother and sister shot back in after her and they all huddled together in the dark little corner, hissing at the strange, frightening noise. The two tabby kittens wriggled and stamped their paws inside a broken wooden crate, making themselves comfy on the old rags and torn-up papers, trying to find the warmest, driest spot. The black-and-white kitten licked them both lovingly, hoping that they'd all curl up together and snooze, as they waited for their mother to come back from her foraging. But the tabby kittens didn't want to hide for long. A minute or so later, they were already nosing out into the alley again.

Their little sister watched them anxiously, wondering about that loud noise and hoping that whatever it was wouldn't come back. The alley was so open—she liked places where she could hide and still see everything. All that space made her nervous.

"Oh, look! Kittens!"

A little boy came running into the alley, and the tabby kittens streaked back toward the old boxes, knocking their black-and-white sister sideways. She huddled at the back of their little den, her heart thumping, but the bravest of the tabbies was too curious to stay hidden, even with the boy blundering around, his feet stamping and thudding. She scrambled out past the broken board onto the top of the box and gazed at him.

"Mom, look...," the little boy whispered. "It really is a kitten! She's tiny!"

"Isn't she? She's beautiful."

The black-and-white kitten squeaked worriedly. There was someone else out there, too. She wished her sister would come back, but now her brother was wriggling out to see what was going on.

"Oh, there's two! Look, Owen, the other one came out to see you. I wonder who they belong to! I guess they're strays, but they look very young. Their mother must be around somewhere."

The voices were soft and gentle, and the black-and-white kitten stretched her paws, shook her whiskers, and began to creep toward the opening. Maybe she would go and see what was happening....

But then the little boy shrieked with laughter as kitten whiskers tickled his fingers. The kitten ran back and buried herself in the rags again. At last she heard their footsteps echoing back down the alley, and she relaxed a bit. Then a tabby-striped face pushed in through the gap between the boxes, and she darted forward to nuzzle happily at her mother. The thin tabby cat had been hiding out of the way until the little boy and his mom were gone. She had always been a stray, and she wasn't very fond of people. People meant food, but sometimes they threw things and shouted at her for pawing around in garbage cans. She avoided them as much as she could.

The tabby kittens piled in after her and tore at the ham sandwich she'd found for them, scrambling and hissing over the delicious pieces of ham. The kittens were eight weeks old, and they were all still drinking her milk as well as eating food, but they were always hungry.

The black-and-white kitten finished her piece of sandwich and snuggled up against her mother. She was warm and safe and full of food. Her brother and sister flopped down on top of her in a softly purring pile of fur, and all four of them curled up to sleep.

"So, how was it?" Grandma asked, smiling at Alicia as they walked home from school on Monday. She didn't need to ask how school had been for Will. He was bouncing around the pavement in front of them with his new best friend, Henry, doing ninja kicks.

"It was okay," Alicia said, not very enthusiastically. It was true. No one had been mean, and she'd understood the work they were doing. Emma, the girl who'd been told to give her a hand, had been nice and had made sure she knew where everything was.

But she'd stayed on the sidelines of all the games. And everyone knew secret jokes about the teachers that she didn't, and there was no one who knew all the fun things about her, the things her friends back home knew. She was just a boring new girl.

Grandma put an arm around her shoulders. "It'll get better, Alicia, I promise. In a month, it won't feel like a new school anymore."

Alicia blinked. She hadn't expected Grandma to notice that she wasn't really happy. "I guess so," she mumbled and smiled gratefully at Grandma.

"Why don't we stop in at the bakery and get a treat? To celebrate school being just about all right?" Grandma suggested.

Will turned around midair and came racing back to them, saying good-bye to Henry. "Cupcakes? Can we? Can I have a marshmallow cream one?"

Grandma made a face. "I guess so. I don't know how you can eat those things, though."

"It's really easy," Will told her solemnly and Alicia giggled, feeling the nervous lump inside her melt away for the first time that day.

It was as they were coming out of the bakery, each clutching a rustling paper bag, that Alicia first saw the kittens. She wondered afterward if they'd heard the bags crinkling, and were hoping that she and Will might drop some food.

She'd seen a flash out of the corner of her eye, a darting movement in the alley. Alicia almost didn't stop to look at first—she'd thought that it was probably just pigeons, hopping around and looking for crumbs—but then something had made her turn back and look more closely.

The soft gray shadows peering out from behind the garbage cans had been cats!

No, kittens. Tiny kittens, two of them, their green eyes round and huge in little striped faces.

Alicia reached out her hand to grab Will, who was explaining very seriously to Grandma that it was important to eat a marshmallow cream cupcake from the bottom up, because then you got to save the marshmallow for last.

"Ow! What?"

"Look...," Alicia whispered, pulling him closer so that he'd see. "But shhh!"

"What am I looking at and you didn't have to grab me, Alicia, Dad says— Oh!"

Grandma peered over their heads. "Please tell me that's not a rat."

"They're kittens, Grandma. Can we go and take a closer look? Please?"

Grandma looked at the shops on either side of the alley. "Well, I don't think they'll mind. Don't go into the yard, though, and don't touch them."

Alicia and Will crept down the alley, holding hands. The little tabby kittens stared at them from behind the garbage cans. They were crouched low to the ground, ready to spring away to safety, but they stayed still as the children came closer.

When they were almost at the garbage cans, Alicia knelt down, gently pulling Will with her.

"Can't we go closer?" he begged.

"Not yet," she whispered back. "When I went to Jenny's house, her cat was really shy, and I had to sit like this for a while, but then he climbed into my lap and let me cuddle him. Jenny says he never does that." Suddenly, Alicia was blinking away tears, thinking of Jenny and all her friends back home.

"They're coming closer." Will poked her arm impatiently. "Look!"

Alicia dragged her hand across her eyes. It was true—one of the kittens had padded all the way out now—and he was almost close enough to sniff at Will's outstretched fingers.

Then, suddenly, he darted forward and dabbed his nose at Will's hand.

Will squeaked delightedly. "His nose is all cold and damp!"

The kitten disappeared back behind the garbage cans in a blur.

"I'm sorry!" Will whispered.

But it only took seconds for the kitten to be brave enough to peek out again, and this time the other tabby kitten followed him, sniffing curiously at Alicia's school shoes.

Very slowly, Alicia reached out and petted the kitten's striped head with the tips of her fingers—the fur was so soft, almost silky. And then the kitten purred, so loudly that Alicia couldn't help giggling. The noise seemed too big for such a tiny creature.

"I wonder where their mother is," Alicia whispered to Will, looking down the alley to see if the mother cat was watching them playing with her babies.

"Are they lost?" Will asked worriedly.

"No," Grandma said quietly behind them. "I was just talking to Emma, the girl from the bakery. She said that they live in the yard—there's a pile of old boxes and things. She's been putting some food out for them."

"They live in a box?" Alicia said, thinking how cold it had been the night before.

Grandma nodded. "Yes. But apparently a couple of her regular customers are thinking of trying to adopt these two once they're big enough to leave their mother. That won't be long."

"Grandma, there's another one!" Alicia gasped. "I was looking for their mom, but there's a kitten peeking out of that old box! A black-and-white one!"

"Yes, there is!" Grandma looked over to where Alicia was pointing. "That's odd. The girl in the bakery only mentioned the two tabbies. Maybe that little one isn't as friendly as the others. I'm sorry, you two, but we have to get going. I need to get dinner ready." She smiled down at Alicia's disappointed face. "I'm sure they'll still be here tomorrow...."

Chapter Three
A New Friend

They were late the next morning because Will had spilled half a bowl of cereal on his school uniform, so there was no time to stop and play with kittens. Alicia looked down the alley hopefully on their way to school, but she couldn't see even a whisker. She imagined all the kittens sleeping in, curled up snugly in their old box.

When they stopped on the way home, Emma, the lady from the bakery, was there, putting some trash out in the garbage cans. She smiled at Alicia and Will and said, "Are you looking for those kittens? I'm really sorry, but that lady I was telling your grandmother about came and took them home with her this morning."

"Oh…." Alicia swallowed. Will's eyes had filled with tears, and she felt like crying, too. She nudged her little brother. "That's good," she said firmly, trying to convince herself as well as Will. "It's getting colder now that it's fall. Imagine sleeping outside in a box all winter."

Grandma nodded. "It would be horrible. Damp and chilly. They're much better off inside in a nice home."

"I know." Will sniffed. "But I wanted to see them. We only got to see them once."

"I'll miss them," Emma said as Alicia and Will turned to go. "Cute little pair. Beautiful stripes."

Alicia glanced back at her. "But—there was a black-and-white kitten, too. Did she take all three of them?"

Emma blinked. "Three? Really? I thought there were only two of them."

"No." Alicia shook her head. "Definitely three. We saw the black-and-white one yesterday."

"She's right," Grandma put in. "I saw her, too. She reminded me of the cat I had when I was a little girl. She was named Catkin. This kitten had the same pretty white tip on her tail."

Alicia glanced at Will in surprise. Grandma had had a cat of her own? Dad had said she didn't like pets.

Will wasn't really listening, though. "Grandma, is the little kitten left all on her own now?"

"Her mom's still there," Emma pointed out.

"No other kittens to play with, though," Alicia said sadly.

Will beamed at her. "Maybe she'll come and play with us instead, then, if she's lonely." He ran a few steps farther down the alley and called, "Here, kitty, kitty!"

"She won't come out if you yell at her," Alicia said. "We have to be gentle. Maybe tempt her out. Could we buy some cat treats, Grandma?"

"I suppose." Grandma nodded. "Maybe if that kitten gets more used to people, someone will take her home, too."

Alicia caught her breath. She almost asked Grandma if they could be the ones to give the kitten a home. But then she remembered everything Dad had said about having to keep the house neat and not damaging Grandma's things and how Grandma hated messes. And then she thought about Jenny's mom rolling her eyes and sighing and saying, "Oh, not again!" when Jenny's cat, Socks, had knocked a vase of flowers off the kitchen table.

There was no way Grandma would let them have a cat, even if the kitten did look like her old pet, Catkin.

A New Friend

Alicia frowned down at her magazine. It was her favorite one, a pet magazine that she got every week. She'd brought it to school to read at recess. Everyone was still being friendly, but she hated having to ask to join in the games. It was embarrassing. It was easier to sit on one of the benches and read.

This week's magazine had a big article on animal charities and an interview with the manager of an ASPCA shelter. She was talking about how important it was to find cats new homes quickly, as they didn't really like being kept all together. They wanted a place to call their own. Alicia sighed to herself as she thought of the black-and-white kitten.

But the really strange thing was that the ASPCA lady also said that black cats and black-and-white ones were much harder to find homes for than tabbies or orange tigers. Alicia just couldn't understand why. The article said that people thought black-and-white cats were too ordinary, not pretty like tabbies.

It made Alicia so angry that she almost tore the page because she was gripping it so tightly. How could people think that? All cats and kittens were different! Jenny's cat Socks was white, with an orange tail and a funny orange stripe down his nose. But that didn't mean he was a better pet than the little black-and-white kitten would be.

The article also said that some people didn't want cats that were black all over because they were worried that they might not be seen on the road and could get run over. *At least that makes sense*, Alicia thought. But they could always get their black cat a reflective collar, couldn't they?

"If I ever get a cat, I'm definitely going to a rescue and choosing a black-and-white one," she said. "Or a pretty black cat. Like a witch's cat."

"Is it good?"

Alicia jumped so hard she almost banged her head on the back of the bench, and the girl leaning over to talk to her gasped.

"I'm sorry! I didn't mean to scare you. I get that magazine sometimes, too. I was just wondering if it was a good one this week."

"Oh!" Alicia nodded and smiled. "Yes. But kind of sad. There's a big article about rescues. And it says not many people choose the black cats. I was just thinking I definitely would."

"Oh, me, too," the other girl agreed.

Alicia thought frantically, trying to remember her name. There were a lot of girls in her class, but she thought this one was named Sarah. "Our cat's mostly black, but he has a white front and white paws. My mom says he looks like he's wearing a penguin suit." She leaned over and looked at the article. "What's that about Black Cat Appreciation Day?"

Alicia looked at the bubble down near the bottom of the page. "It's to show everyone that black cats are special. It's in August here, but it says in England, it's in October—oh, the same day as Halloween. I guess that makes sense. But black cats aren't all spooky."

Sarah giggled. "They're good at appearing out of nowhere, though. I'm always tripping over Harvey."

"Aw, that's such a cute name for a cat." Alicia smiled.

"He just looks like a Harvey," Sarah explained. "Even when he was a kitten, there was something Harvey-ish about him. Do you have a cat?" she added, looking at Alicia sideways. There was something hopeful about the way she asked it, as though she wanted someone to share cat stories with. A friend who had a cat of her own—what could be better than that?

It was the first time someone had really seemed interested in her at school. If she said no, Sarah would shrug and smile and walk away, Alicia was sure of it. And she was just as sure that she didn't want that to happen. So she nodded, slowly, trying to think about what to say. "Yes. We have a kitten." She slipped her hand under the magazine and crossed her fingers. She hated to lie, especially to someone as nice as Sarah, but she had to. "We just got her." It was almost true, wasn't it? She wanted that little black-and-white kitten from the alley to be theirs, so much....

"Oh, you're so lucky! Is she pretty? What does she look like? How old is she?"

Alicia swallowed. "She's black-and-white, like Harvey. And she's very little, just old enough to leave her mother. She was a stray."

"What's her name?" Sarah demanded eagerly.

Alicia blinked. She couldn't think. Not a single name would come into her head. What was a good name for a kitten?

Then she smiled at Sarah. She knew the perfect name.

"Her name is Catkin."

Chapter Four
The Visitor

"What's the matter, Alicia?" Grandma looked up from her book and peered across the table at her granddaughter's pile of books. "You haven't written anything in a while."

"It's a project." Alicia sighed. "It's hard. It's about Egyptians, and we can make the project about whatever we want—that's what's so hard about it.

I can't choose, even though I've got all these books from the library."

And, of course, only half her mind was on her project. The rest of it was worrying about having lied to Sarah two days ago. Especially since Sarah was really, really excited. She kept asking about Catkin, and she obviously really wanted to come and see her. But she was too nice—or maybe too shy—to come right out and ask if she could come over. Alicia had a feeling that she was working herself up to it, though.

The awful thing was, Alicia would have liked Sarah to come over. She'd love to have a friend come over to play. Grandma and Dad kept gently asking if there was anyone she really liked at school and if she wanted to invite somebody over. Will had had Henry come over and had been over to his house, too. And he'd been invited to a birthday party already.

But if Sarah came over, she'd know that Alicia had been lying about Catkin and she'd hate her. She might even tell the entire class that Alicia was a liar.

"I went to Egypt, you know," Grandma said thoughtfully, breaking into Alicia's thoughts. "It must have been, oh, goodness, eight, ten years ago? Yes, just before you were born, Alicia. I went to see the pyramids with one of my friends from school, Aunt Barbara. Do you remember her?"

Alicia didn't, but she nodded as if she did. "You really went there? What was it like? Did you go and see the Great Pyramid?"

"We certainly did. We went inside it, too. It was pretty scary," Grandma added slowly. "Very shadowy, and it was hard to breathe. I have to admit that I didn't like it much, Alicia, but I'm glad I saw it. And from the outside, the pyramids were incredible to look at. Wait a minute." She smiled and got up, walking into the living room. Alicia could hear her opening drawers in the big display cabinet that had most of her precious, breakable possessions in it.

Grandma came back in, carefully unrolling a piece of brownish paper. "This is what I brought back as a souvenir of the vacation, Alicia. It's a papyrus. Like paper, but made out of reeds." She held it out. "You can take a look."

Alicia looked at her uncertainly. "Isn't it fragile?" she asked worriedly. She wanted to hold it—she could see that the painting on it was beautiful, a black cat wearing a jeweled necklace and even an earring, it looked like.

"I know you'll be careful." Grandma smiled at her. "I should get it framed, really. It's such a beautiful painting. The box on the side says my name in hieroglyphics. I watched the man doing it."

Alicia took the papyrus, feeling the roughness against her fingers. She could even see the lines of the reed stems in the weave. "The cat is so beautiful," she said. Then she grinned up at Grandma. "I can't see many cats agreeing to wear all that jewelry, though. Most of them don't even like collars!"

Grandma nodded. "But this one is a goddess. Her name is Bast."

Alicia examined the picture again. "There was a cat goddess? Wow.... Grandma, I could do my project on her!" Very carefully, she laid the papyrus down on the table so she could fling her arms around her grandmother.

"Maybe I could even copy the painting!"

As she hugged Grandma tightly, Alicia realized something else. Grandma couldn't possibly dislike cats that much, could she? Not when she'd chosen a painting of a cat as a special souvenir.

The black-and-white kitten was enjoying a patch of sunlight in the yard. Her mother was off looking for food, and the little kitten was stretched out, snoozing, with her nose on her paws.

Her ears fluttered a little as she heard a noise coming from the back of one of the shops, and then her eyes flew open. Someone was coming!

She darted back into the safety of the box, her heart thudding fast against her ribs. The voices were loud, frightening even, and there were heavy feet clumping all around her.

She pressed herself back into the corner of the box, thinking that they would just dump their garbage in the cans and go. But no one usually came close to the pile of old boxes like this. It wasn't a delivery—no van had driven down the alley. She was almost used to that noise, although she still didn't like it.

This was something different. And then suddenly the box, her safe, warm box, shifted and split, and she let out a high-pitched squeak of fright. What was happening?

"There's something in there," a deep voice growled. "Ugh, not rats, I hope."

"I don't think so—there's a stray cat that hangs around the yard. Maybe it's her."

Someone clapped his hands loudly, the sound sharp and echoing in the enclosed yard. "Go on, shoo! Get lost, cat!"

The kitten squeaked again, and her box tipped sideways. She shot out, terrified, and streaked across the yard, away from the growling voices.

"There she goes—but that's just a kitten. Not much bigger than a rat, poor little thing!"

The kitten huddled in the corner, panicking. Someone was coming toward her, huge boots thumping. She had never tried to climb the fences before, but anything was better than staying here. She sank her claws in the wood and scrambled frantically upward, balancing for a moment on the very top of the fence. Then she jumped down the other side and set off through the bushes, to who knew where.

Alicia was stretched out in the long grass, idly picking the blades. She'd done her homework and typed up a lot of work for her project on the computer. She felt relaxed and happy in the autumn sun. Grandma had given her a sandwich to keep her going until Dad got home and they could all have dinner together, but Alicia hadn't finished it—she was feeling too lazy even to eat.

She could hear Will at the end of the yard, humming to himself as he investigated the greenhouse. Grandma didn't use it very much these days and some of the glass panes were broken, but Dad had told them he'd plant seeds in the springtime. He'd already cleaned up part of the yard closest to the house, but Alicia and Will loved this wild part, with the overgrown bushes. It was full of hidden nests and little dark caves. Alicia glanced sideways, checking that the big spotted garden spider hanging off the branch by her foot hadn't moved. She didn't mind him being there—he'd probably lived here longer than she had—but she didn't want him getting any closer.

He was still there. But underneath him, peering out at her from the shadows, was a tiny black-and-white face.

A kitten! The same kitten she had seen in the alley, Alicia was almost sure. She looked across the yard at the greenhouse and the fence. She hadn't realized before, but the shops were very close to Grandma's backyard, even though to get to them by the street, you had to go a long way around.

"Did you climb over the fence?" Alicia whispered, very, very quietly.

The kitten stared back at her. *She's so small and thin*, Alicia thought. She looked exhausted—as though she was frightened, but too worn out even to run.

Slowly, creeping her fingers across the grass, Alicia stretched out a hand to get her sandwich. It was chicken. Perfect for a kitten treat.

The kitten watched her, wide-eyed, shrinking back a little as Alicia's hand came close. But then she smelled the chicken—Alicia could see the exact moment. Her whiskers twitched and her ears flicked forward, then her eyes grew even rounder.

Alicia tore off a tiny piece of sandwich and gently laid it down, just where the tufts of long grass met the branches.

Then she watched. The kitten didn't have to move far. If she wasn't brave enough, maybe Alicia could throw her a piece farther in, but that might scare her away.

The kitten looked at the piece of sandwich, and Alicia could see her sniffing. She looked between Alicia and the sandwich a few times, then she wriggled forward on her stomach, inching slowly toward the food. As soon as she was close enough, she seized the yummy mouthful and darted back into the safety of the bush.

Alicia wanted to laugh, but she folded her lips together firmly in case the noise scared the kitten away. She watched the kitten wolf down the scrap, and then she tore off a little more. This time she left it a little closer to her feet.

The kitten didn't take as long to decide if she was going for the food the second time. She gave Alicia one slightly suspicious look and then raced to grab it.

After that, Alicia put the plate down, right next to her feet, to see what would happen. Surely the kitten wouldn't be able to drag away a whole sandwich, would she? She'd have to stop by the plate and eat it there. And then maybe Alicia would be able to pet her....

The kitten stared at the sandwich. The two pieces she'd already eaten had been so delicious. But now the rest of the sandwich was closer to the girl, and she wasn't sure that she was brave enough to go and take it.

But the smell.... She could still taste it in her mouth, and she was really hungry. She hadn't eaten in such a long time. After she had scrambled over the fence the afternoon before, she had run and climbed and run again, frightened and desperate to get away. Her cozy den in the box had suddenly been snatched from her, and she didn't understand. She just knew that she wasn't safe there anymore.

She had only stopped in the big yard because she was tired. Wriggling through the tiny gap under the back fence had worn her out. She had simply lain down in the dry, shadowy space under the bush and gone to sleep. When she'd woken, it had been dark, and she had been so hungry. She'd finally understood that everything was different now. Her mother wasn't there to bring her food, and there was no one there to curl up and sleep with. She was lost and all alone.

She had been on her own before, of course. But she had always known that her mother would come back. The kitten would purr throatily, and her mother would wash her, licking her fur lovingly all over.

Now her fur was dusty and matted with dirt, and a clump of it had torn out when she had squeezed under the fence. She had sat there below the bush and tried to wash herself, but it wasn't the same, and it only made her feel more lonely.

The night sounds seemed louder than they'd ever been before. Cars roared past and made her shudder with fright, and people laughed and shouted. Another cat had stalked through the yard, late at night, but it hadn't been her mother. She had jumped up eagerly, ready to run and nuzzle it, but all it had done was stare at her, and she'd seen it fluff out its tail. Then it had walked along the side of the house, and the kitten had ducked back under the bush, knowing that she was more lost than ever.

As Alicia pursed her lips and tried to call to the kitten using sounds that she thought she would like, the kitten stared back at her and wondered what to do. The girl seemed quiet and gentle, not like those stomping men who had chased her away from her home. And she had food. Right now, food seemed to be the most important thing of all.

Slowly, paw by paw, the kitten came

out of her hiding place and crept toward Alicia.

Chapter Five
A Plan

"Alicia…."

"*Shhh!*"

"Alicia, is that a kitten? Is that the kitten from near the bakery?"

"Yes, but *shhh!* Please don't make her run away. She's really shy, Will. Come and sit down."

Will sat down, as slowly and quietly as he could, and stared at the kitten.

She stared back for a moment, but she was so busy devouring the rest of the chicken sandwich that she didn't really have time to worry about him.

"How did she get here?"

"I don't know." Alicia reached out one hand and held it by the plate, close enough for the kitten to sniff. The kitten glared at her and then butted gently at Alicia's hand.

Will giggled. "She's telling you to get off her sandwich."

"Maybe. Or she might be putting her scent on me," said Alicia. "That's what a cat is doing when it rubs its face against you. They have scent glands there. They're saying we belong to them."

I want to belong to you, she added silently. *Please stay. Please, please, please.*

"Alicia," Will whispered. "Do you think—do you think she could be our cat? Can we keep her?" He looked around the yard. "We could make her a bed in the greenhouse. Wow, she actually finished all of that sandwich. Do you think she wants another one? Grandma asked if I wanted a sandwich but I said no. I could go and say that I've changed my mind...."

Alicia looked worried. "I don't like

telling Grandma lies—but we can't tell her the truth, can we? Dad said she wouldn't want a pet in the house. And this kitten really needs food. She's so skinny."

"The greenhouse isn't in the house!" Will said with a grin. "So we could just forget to tell her, it doesn't matter."

Alicia couldn't help thinking that it did matter, and that they were just twisting things around to be the way they wanted—but she wouldn't be able to handle it if Grandma made them take the kitten back to the alley. The greenhouse would be like a palace to a kitten who was used to living in a box. And Grandma didn't usually go down to the far end of the yard. It would be all right.

And if she really had a kitten, she wouldn't be lying to Sarah anymore.

"Yes." She nodded. "Go and ask Grandma if you can have a sandwich. With lots of chicken."

"Oh, dear, what's the matter with that poor little girl?" Grandma sped up as they made their way home from school. She hurried down the pavement toward a toddler standing outside the bakery next to a little scooter and howling. "I hope she's not lost."

"She isn't, Grandma. Look, I can see her mom coming." Alicia pointed to a lady running toward the little girl.

"Good." Grandma bent over the little

girl. "What happened, sweetheart? Did you fall off your scooter?"

The little girl stared back at her and shook her head. She stopped crying.

Grandma smiled at the little girl's mother, who had reached them at last and was now crouched next to her daughter, hugging her and all out of breath. "I'm sorry," Grandma began. "We didn't see what happened, but she says she didn't fall."

"Mommy! The cat!" And the little girl began to howl again.

"Oh, Megan! Did you try and pet a cat? Did he scratch you?"

The little girl nodded and wailed louder, holding up her arm toward her mom.

Alicia sucked in her breath through

her teeth—Megan had a long scratch down the inside of her arm. It wasn't bleeding very much, but it obviously hurt.

"Some cats are just grumpy, Megan. You know I said not to chase them." Her mom sighed. "Don't worry, baby. We'll go home and put some medicine on it."

Alicia bit her lip. It probably wasn't the right time to say that the cat must have been scared if the little girl had tried to grab it.

"It was probably that stray tabby that lives down at the end of the alley," Grandma said. "Stray cats can be very wild and fierce."

Alicia and Will exchanged glances, thinking of the little black-and-white kitten, curled up in the greenhouse back at home. They'd made her a cozy bed out of one of the cardboard boxes they'd had for packing up their things, tipped on its side and lined with an old sweatshirt of Alicia's. Then they'd put out a trail of chicken sandwich pieces to show the kitten where the greenhouse was.

Alicia and Will had done their best to make it into the nicest den a kitten could have. They'd even made her a litter box out of an old seed tray they'd found on one of the greenhouse shelves—it had been full of dusty earth. Alicia had a feeling the kitten might not know what it was for, since she was a stray and was used to going to the bathroom anywhere, but if she was going to be an indoor cat one day, it was important to try. Will had brought her a small saucer full of water from the outside faucet, too.

That morning, before they went to school, Alicia had snuck outside with some cereal and milk. It wasn't the best thing for a kitten, she knew, but they didn't have any cat food. Anyway, the kitten hadn't seemed to mind. She had buried her face in it eagerly, and when Alicia finally had to go, the kitten had been blissfully licking milky bits off her whiskers.

She hadn't looked very wild and fierce at all. She was still shy, of course. But when Alicia had arrived with the bowl, she hadn't run away, or hidden herself behind the wobbly towers of flowerpots. Instead, she'd just pricked her ears, wary, but hopeful.

Alicia and Will lagged behind Grandma for the rest of the way home.

"Did you hear what Grandma said about stray cats being fierce?" Will asked anxiously.

Alicia nodded. "I know. I was really wishing we could tell her about Catkin."

"Catkin?" Will blinked in surprise. "You named her?" He frowned a little. Alicia could tell he was hurt that she'd given the kitten a name without talking to him.

"Grandma used to have a black-and-white cat named Catkin," Alicia explained. "She was telling me about her. It's a really sweet name, and I thought that maybe if we called the kitten Catkin, too, it would remind her of it. But now Grandma is thinking about mean, fierce cats instead. It's the worst timing ever."

"Ohhh." Will nodded. "I see. But our Catkin is sweet, Alicia. She's not fierce at all. Grandma will see that, won't she?"

"I think so. But let's not tell her just yet that we've got Catkin in the greenhouse. She'll have to go on being our secret kitten. And don't tell Dad, either!"

"Come on, you two!" Grandma called back. "It's starting to rain."

Alicia and Will sped up, the first fat drops splashing onto the pavement as they dashed after Grandma.

"What if she gets wet?" Will hissed. "The greenhouse has all those big holes in the roof! She'll get wet for sure!"

"You're right," Alicia muttered back. She smiled at Will. "You know that big old wardrobe in my bedroom....

Maybe we could hide her in there."

"Why not in my bedroom?" Will said.

"Because you don't have a wardrobe, just drawers. And because your bedroom is next to Dad's! Mine's up those creaky stairs, and I can always hear people coming. So I've got time to hide a kitten in my wardrobe before they get to the top, you see?"

"I guess so." Will sighed heavily.

Alicia smiled to herself, imagining falling asleep tonight with the faint sound of purring echoing out from her wardrobe. Or maybe even a small furry ball of kitten on the end of her bed. "I hope she understands we're trying to help," Alicia said suddenly. "She might not want to come inside. She's probably never been in a house before."

Alicia had thought they'd be able to tempt Catkin inside gradually. She'd never thought of doing it so soon.

Will grinned at her. "I think if you gave her a chicken sandwich, she'd probably go anywhere!"

Chapter Six
A Big Secret

"Distract Grandma! Show her your cut knee," Alicia muttered, thinking of Megan and her scratch. She had the wet kitten and her old sweatshirt bundled up in her arms, and there was a lot of squeaking and wriggling going on. She'd taken the cheese from her lunch box (she'd saved it on purpose), and they'd snuck outside while

Grandma was taking off her coat and changing into her slippers. Catkin had been so excited about the cheese that she'd hardly minded when Alicia had picked her up. But now Alicia needed to get upstairs quickly. "Go in the bathroom…. Pretend you're looking for the first-aid box. Quick!" The armful of sweatshirt was wriggling like crazy. "It's all right, Catkin. Just a tiny bit longer."

Will ran in through the back door and then into the bathroom. If he could get Grandma to follow him in there, she wouldn't see Alicia dash past.

"Grandma! My knee's bleeding! Can you get me a bandage? I fell down at school."

Alicia could hear Grandma bustling through the kitchen and then the squeak of the bathroom door. It was on Dad's DIY list to oil that door, so she was glad he hadn't done it yet. Huddling Catkin close, she darted through the kitchen, into the hallway, and up the stairs.

Up in her room, she kicked the door gently shut and put her bundle down on the floor. Catkin shook her way out of the sweatshirt looking indignant and hissed faintly at Alicia.

"I'm sorry," Alicia whispered back.
"I couldn't let Grandma see you. And
it's really pouring out there now. I bet
your box is soggy already. I'll make you
a new bed. Look."

She grabbed another cardboard box
off the teetering pile in the corner of her
room and put it sideways in the bottom
of her wardrobe, shoving all her shoes
to one side. Catkin was still standing
on the sweatshirt, so Alicia made a nest
shape out of her woolly winter scarf and
put that in the box instead. Then she put
the last piece of cheese down in front of
the box, too. It was still sitting in one
of Grandma's little plastic containers,

which made a perfect cat-food bowl.

"I'll get you some water in a minute," Alicia promised. "And the litter box. Your things are just outside the back door. Will brought them in from the greenhouse."

She looked at the kitten home thoughtfully and then at Catkin, who had slunk under her bed. The kitten looked worried.

"I know it's strange," Alicia told her quietly. "But we're nice. Really. And there's more cheese." She tapped her fingernails against the wardrobe door to make Catkin look and then tipped up the plastic container to show her. "Did you want another chicken sandwich instead? Are they your favorite? They're my favorite, too."

Catkin edged out from under the bed, sniffing. She was confused. But she had never had so much food before—her brother and sister had always fought for more of their mother's milk and the same with the scraps. It wasn't just the sandwiches and the cereal or the cheese, either—the two children had been so gentle. Alicia and Will had whispered to her and tried to purr at her, and that morning, Alicia had run one finger softly all down her back, which had tickled. It had been strange and different, but she had liked it. And now there was another soft box bed and more food. She liked being inside, all warm and dry. So she padded cautiously across the room and stopped to sniff at Alicia's fingers. Then she butted her head up against Alicia's hand and went to nibble daintily at the cheese in the container.

Alicia sat watching her, smiling to herself. Her own kitten. In her own bedroom. Almost, anyway.

Then she froze. The steps up to her room were creaking. She was just sitting forward, ready to scoop Catkin farther into the wardrobe and close the door, when she heard Will hissing, "It's only me! I've got the litter box!"

Alicia wriggled back slowly and went to open the door. "Wow! How did you do that?"

"Grandma's on the phone with Aunt Susie. She'll be a while. Angel Katie did really well at her ballet performance." Angel Katie was what they called their little cousin. "Grandma was in the living room, and she didn't see me at all. I've got the water, too."

"That's great. If I move my shoes and put them under my desk instead, we can put the litter box in the corner of the wardrobe. And this newspaper I used to wrap my photo frames can go underneath, just in case. Don't worry, Catkin. We're just making it nice for you."

"I hope she understands what to do," Will said doubtfully. "What if she pees in the wrong place? Like, I don't know, in your slippers?"

Alicia grinned at him. "Yuck. But actually, I don't think I'd mind. She's only little. I remember when you were a baby and you peed in Dad's face when he was changing your diaper."

Will turned red. "No, you don't! You can't remember that. You were little yourself."

"Well, I remember Dad telling me about it once, anyway. I bet Catkin won't make as much mess as a baby."

Catkin finished the cheese and sniffed thoughtfully at the litter box. Then she snuggled up on Alicia's scarf and pulled the sweater over herself, almost like a blanket. She tucked her nose comfortably under her tail, and as the two children watched, she fell fast asleep.

"I hope Grandma didn't go into your room for anything today," Will whispered to Alicia as they hurried across the playground the next afternoon. It was Friday, and everyone was running and swinging their bags, eager to get home and start the weekend.

"Me, too. But I don't think she would have. I took all of my dirty clothes downstairs and put them in the washing machine for her. And Dad vacuumed my room a couple of days ago. Catkin was really good last night. She didn't meow or anything, and she even used the litter box. This morning she was sitting on my windowsill when I woke up, just looking out the window." Alicia crossed her fingers. "Look, there's Grandma by the gate. She doesn't look angry, does she? Not like someone who's found a kitten in a wardrobe." They waved to Grandma and she waved back, smiling.

Just then someone called out her name. "Alicia!" It was Sarah.

Alicia swung around and beamed at her friend. "Hello!"

"Alicia, can I ask you a big favor?" Sarah said pleadingly, as they walked toward the gate. "I live near you, you know. Just a couple of streets down. Do you think I could stop by your house for five minutes on the way home? Just to see your kitten? Pleeease? My mom said it was fine if you said I could."

Alicia stopped walking and swallowed hard. She really wanted to say yes.

Maybe she could even tell Sarah the secret. But there wasn't time. Grandma would hear them, because she was really close. In fact, she was coming toward them, smiling. She was probably about to invite Sarah to come over and play.

"I-I can't today…," Alicia whispered, her eyes darting sideways at Grandma. "I've got—dance class." Grandma had been talking about signing her up for dance classes—there were some at the church hall, not far away. It was the first thing that came into her head.

It was a shame that Will blurted out, "I've got to go to soccer!" at the same time.

"We've got both," Alicia said hurriedly. "Friday just isn't a good day."

Grandma was standing next to them

now, looking curious, and Alicia could see Sarah's mom coming over, too.

"If you don't want me to come—" Sarah started to say, sounding a little hurt.

"It isn't that! I do want you to, I really do!"

"You just had to say no—I thought we were friends!"

"We are!" Alicia said anxiously. "It's just—not today. Another day!"

Sarah nodded, but she still looked really disappointed. She grabbed her mom's hand and pulled her away down the street, leaving Alicia and Will and Grandma staring at each other in confusion.

"Alicia, what's the matter? Wasn't that Sarah, the nice girl who lives on Timber Trail? Did you have a fight with her?"

"Yes." Alicia sniffed. "She wanted to come to our house."

"Well, why didn't you let her? She could have had dinner with us."

"It wasn't that. I can't explain. Please can we go home?" Alicia reached out and took Grandma's hand. "Please."

"All right." But Grandma still sounded worried, and she held on to

Alicia's hand as they walked. Alicia could tell she hadn't finished asking about what had happened. "Alicia, was Sarah asking about a kitten?" she said at last as they walked past the alley. "I thought I heard her say something about visiting a kitten…."

Alicia swallowed. "But we don't have a kitten," she pointed out, trying to sound cheerful.

"Alicia…." Grandma pulled her hand gently to make her stop. "Go on ahead for a minute, Will. Here, you can take my keys. Go and open the front door. We'll follow you." She watched as Will walked on ahead and then she followed, walking along slowly with Alicia's hand held tight in hers. "Alicia, did you tell Sarah you had a kitten?"

Alicia didn't say anything. How could she explain?

Grandma went on thoughtfully. "Sometimes it's hard, when you really want to make friends—you make up stories. Little stories to make yourself sound more interesting. Everyone does it sometimes, Alicia. It's all right."

Alicia gaped up at her. "How did you know?"

"Like I said, everyone does it. But almost everyone gets caught, too, sweetie. You're going to have to explain to Sarah and say you're sorry, you know."

Alicia kicked at the pavement with her foot. "I know," she muttered. But inside she was saying, *I didn't make it up. It wasn't a lie. Well, it was when I first said it. But now I'm lying to you instead.... I wish we had told you about Catkin in the first place. What am I going to do?*

"Are you that desperate for a kitten?" Grandma asked suddenly.

Alicia blinked, shocked out of her worries. "Um. I would love one. But Dad said you didn't like pets. Because they were dirty."

Grandma sniffed. "Well, I do like everything to be clean," she agreed. "But a little cat.... Maybe we could think about it."

Alicia swallowed hard and tried to smile. Somehow she had to explain to Grandma that they had a little cat already....

When they got back to the house,

Grandma made hot chocolate, and she even put marshmallows on the top as a treat. She let Alicia and Will take it upstairs, although she did say they had to be careful not to spill any.

"Dinner will be ready in about an hour," she reminded them. "Your dad's working late tonight, so we're not waiting for him today."

Alicia and Will carried the hot chocolate upstairs to Alicia's room, with the sandwiches they'd saved from lunch. At the top of the steps, outside the door, they stopped and looked at each other worriedly. Somehow Alicia felt convinced that the kitten wouldn't be there. Maybe they had imagined it all. She reached out and turned the handle, peering cautiously around the door.

Over in the wardrobe, the kitten lifted her head and yawned. Then she looked up at them and nosed at the empty bowl, clearly hoping for some food.

"Hello," Alicia whispered, starting to shred up her sandwich. "Did you miss us?"

Catkin yawned again and, very faintly, Alicia heard her purr.

"You're happy to see us! You're actually purring. Oh, Catkin. If only we could show you to Grandma right now. I'm sure she'd want to keep you." She patted Catkin's head, loving the feeling of the silky fur under her fingers. "This weekend, somehow, we'll find a way to tell her. We have to."

Chapter Seven
Missing!

When Alicia and Will's dad got home late that night, he sat across the kitchen table from their grandma, eating his dinner.

"What's the matter?" he asked as he wiped a piece of bread around his plate to mop up the gravy. "You've hardly said anything since I got home, Mom."

Grandma sighed and put down her

cup of tea. "I'm just a little worried about Alicia. I'm not sure she's settling in all that well with the other girls at school. She had an argument with one of them this afternoon just as I was picking her up. She didn't want to talk about it very much, but it seems as though she'd told this girl—Sarah is her name—that we had a kitten."

Dad stared at her. "But why on earth would she say that?"

Grandma shrugged. "To fit in? To make herself sound more exciting? We're asking a lot of them, you know, starting at a new school."

Dad's shoulders slumped. "I guess so. But I thought it was the best thing to do...."

"I still think it is." Grandma reached over and patted his hand. "But I'm wondering if a pet would help Alicia settle in better."

"You don't like pets!"

"What gave you that idea? I wouldn't want a dog—I couldn't manage the walking—but I love cats!" Grandma smiled at him, a little sadly. "Actually, I suppose we didn't have any pets when you were younger, did we? I haven't had a cat of my own for a long time.

Not since Catkin died. She was 20, and I'd had her since I was a little girl. I didn't want another cat for a while after that, and somehow then it just never seemed to be the right time. But I wouldn't mind a cat now. Especially with Alicia and Will to help take care of it."

"Well, it would be wonderful for Alicia," Dad agreed. "I always said no before, because we were out of the house all the time." He got up and took his plate over to the dishwasher. "I'll go and check on her. I know she'll probably be asleep, but I just want to make sure that she's all right…."

Catkin woke up as the morning light shone into Alicia's room. She didn't have any blinds on the windows yet, and the morning was bright and sunny. The kitten stretched blissfully, padding her paws into a patch of sun just outside the wardrobe. Then she hunched up the other way, arching her back, and stepped delicately out into Alicia's bedroom.

Alicia was still fast asleep, huddled under her comforter, so Catkin jumped up onto the bed to sniff at her. She smelled interesting, like breakfast and warm sunshine. But she didn't wake up when Catkin dabbed a chilly nose against her ear—only muttered and turned over, which made the comforter shift alarmingly. Catkin jumped down before she slid off and sat on the rug.

When she'd washed her ears
thoroughly, both sides, Catkin stalked
off across the room. Something was
different, and she hadn't quite figured
out what it was. There was something
in the air, something fresh and new.

The door was open!

Alicia had shut it carefully, of course,
when she came upstairs to go to bed.

But then her dad had come up to check on her. Catkin and Alicia had both been fast asleep, and neither of them had seen that he had left the door ajar. Just wide enough for a small, determined paw to hook it open.

Catkin nosed her way out and started to hop carefully—front feet, then back feet—down the stairs. It felt unfamiliar. Then she trotted along the landing, sniffing curiously at the different doors. She padded into Will's room, but a wobbly pile of books slid over when she nudged it, so she darted out again and set off down the next flight of stairs to the bottom. She sniffed her way carefully down the hallway and into the kitchen.

Most of the food was put away in

cupboards, but Dad had left a loaf of bread out on the counter, and Catkin could smell it. She sat on the floor, staring up and thinking....

Alicia woke up when the sunny patch from the window moved around onto her bed. She blinked sleepily, wondering why it was that she felt so happy and scared all at the same time. Then she sat up straight, remembering.

Catkin!

Today they *had* to find a way to tell Grandma and Dad what had happened, and make them see that Catkin needed to stay with them.

The kitten wasn't sitting on the

windowsill the way she had been the day before, so Alicia kneeled up in bed and leaned over to peer into the wardrobe. "Catkin," she called. "Here, little kitten!"

But no little kitten face appeared, and Alicia's heart began to beat faster. "Where did you go?" she muttered. She hopped out of bed and crouched down to check underneath, but there was nothing there except dust. No Catkin hiding in the cardboard boxes, or behind the little bookshelf by the door.

The open door.

Alicia gasped. "I shut it!" she whispered to herself. "I know I did. Oh, no." She hurried down the stairs, going as fast as she could on tiptoe, so she wouldn't wake Dad or Grandma. She dashed into Will's room.

"Wake up! Will, wake up! Have you seen Catkin? I don't know where she is."

Will stared at her sleepily, blinking like an owl, and then he squeaked and jumped out of bed.

"Where would she go?"

"Shhh! I don't know, maybe the kitchen?"

Will nodded. "Definitely the kitchen."

They hurried down the stairs, freezing every time one of them creaked. The house was old, and they hadn't had time to learn which stairs to step over.

"Dad will hear us," Alicia whispered miserably. "We have to find her and get her back into my room." She kneeled down on the kitchen floor, looking around. She hadn't noticed how many tiny, kitten-sized hiding places there were in here before. On the chairs, under the table. Down the side of the oven. "Oh! What if she climbed into the washing machine?" Alicia gasped. "I read about a cat who did that once."

But the washing machine was empty, and so were all the other spots they could think of. Alicia sat down on the

117

floor, looking helpless. "I can't think of anywhere else," she said. "All the windows are closed, aren't they?"

Will nodded. "It was cold last night. Unless—Grandma always sleeps with her bedroom window open."

A large tear spilled down the side of Alicia's nose. "Maybe she went out that way, then. She didn't want to stay. Catkin's gone!"

Chapter Eight
The Best Day

"What's the matter with you two? Why are you up at seven o'clock on a Saturday morning?" Grandma demanded. She was standing in the kitchen doorway, wrapped in her robe. "Alicia, you're crying! What's wrong?" She put her arms around Alicia, pulling her up from the floor.

"We've lost her!" Alicia sobbed into

Grandma's shoulder. She didn't care about keeping Catkin a secret anymore. It was too late now.

"Lost who?" Grandma stared at Alicia, puzzled, and so did Dad, who'd come in behind her, looking sleepy.

"Catkin," Will explained, coming to lean against Dad's robe. "Our kitten. Alicia found her in the yard. She was in Alicia's wardrobe, but when we woke up, she was gone."

"You had a kitten shut in your wardrobe?" Dad said slowly.

"Not shut in," Alicia shook her head, gulping back tears. "Just her bed was in there and her litter box. She could go anywhere in my room. We couldn't leave her in the greenhouse—the glass is full of holes, and it was pouring on Thursday night."

Dad and Grandma looked shocked. "But what were you feeding her?" Grandma asked, frowning.

"Sandwiches, mostly. She loves chicken." Alicia sniffed. "Just like me. We saved some of our lunches for her, and she was getting tame. We thought she was going to stay with us, but now she's run away. She must have gone through your window, Grandma. It's the only one that was open." Alicia slumped down on one of the kitchen chairs.

Grandma moved slowly over to the counter to put the kettle on, wiping away the breadcrumbs and pushing shut a half-open drawer on the way. "I need a cup of tea," she said. "A kitten in your wardrobe...."

"Where did she come from in the first place? That's what I want to know," Dad said, sitting down across from Alicia with Will on his knee.

"The alley down by the bakery," Alicia explained tiredly. "There were three of them—the two tabbies got adopted, but nobody cared about the little black-and-white kitten. And then she just showed up in our yard."

"And you named her Catkin? Like my Catkin?" Grandma asked, getting mugs out of the cupboard.

"You said your kitten was black-and-white, too," Alicia explained. "And it's a sweet name. It was just right."

"Oh, dear," Grandma sighed. "Maybe she was just too wild to be a pet, Alicia. If she's never really known people...."

"But she wasn't wild," Alicia tried to explain. She could feel herself starting to cry again. "She was shy, but she purred at us. And she loved our food, even if she didn't really love us yet."

"Well, maybe we could go back to the alley by the shops and look for her," Grandma said thoughtfully, leaning over to get a clean dish towel out of the drawer.

"You mean—if we found her, we could bring her back home again?" Alicia gasped. "We can keep her?" She jumped up. "Can we go over there now?"

Will wriggled off Dad's knee. "Right now?"

But Grandma was standing staring into the dish towel drawer. "I don't think we need to…. Look."

Alicia leaned over and clapped her hand across her mouth. Curled up among Grandma's neatly stacked dish towels was a black-and-white kitten, half-asleep and blinking up at them in confusion.

"I shut the drawer…," Grandma said. "When I went to make the tea. It was open, just a little. You know how that drawer sticks sometimes...."

"Just enough for a skinny kitten to climb in, but not enough for us to see her!" Alicia said, her eyes wide.

Sleepily, Catkin stared up at Alicia and Grandma and let out a little purr. Maybe there was going to be food. The bread seemed like a long time ago, and it had been a lot of effort to get up onto the counter and steal a slice. She was hungry again.

"What a sweetheart," Grandma said, laughing as Catkin stepped carefully out of her nest in the drawer. She rubbed her furry face against Grandma's hand and purred even louder. "Just like my Catkin," Grandma said, petting her ears. "You're staying now, aren't you?"

Catkin jumped down to the floor and wove her way around Grandma's ankles and then Alicia's, still purring.

"That means yes," Alicia whispered. "I know it does."

"You actually had her hidden in your wardrobe?" Sarah asked Alicia again as they followed Grandma home from school on Monday afternoon. "You had a secret kitten?"

"Yes. And I really wanted you to see her, but I couldn't let Grandma find out. Or I thought I couldn't. It turns out we probably should have just told her to start with."

"That wouldn't have been as exciting," Sarah said, shaking her head.

"No." Alicia smiled at her. "It *was* wonderful, Catkin being our secret. But now we can play with her without worrying about Dad and Grandma. And she still likes my bedroom best in all of the house."

"Should we stop and buy some cupcakes, girls?" Grandma suggested as they reached the bakery. "Oh, Will, come back!"

Alicia and Sarah giggled as Will raced ahead, flinging open the door of the bakery. When they caught up with him, he was already telling Emma, who was behind the counter, that he wanted a marshmallow cream cupcake.

"You know the black-and-white

kitten, the one that was living in your yard?" Alicia said shyly to Emma after they'd chosen their cupcakes. "She came into our yard, and we're going to keep her!"

Emma smiled delightedly. "Oh, that's such good news! I looked for her, after you two told me she was there, but I never saw her. I did wonder if you'd imagined her."

"No, she's just a little shy." Alicia smiled to herself, remembering Catkin running madly around the kitchen after a ping-pong ball that morning and then collapsing in her lap, exhausted, with her paws in the air. She wasn't shy with them, not anymore.

"I've got news for you, too," Emma went on as she put their chocolate cupcakes into a bag. "I called the cat rescue about the kittens' mom to ask them what the best thing was to do. They're going to catch her and spay her so she doesn't have more kittens. They said she probably won't ever be tame enough to be a housecat, but if she's not trying to feed kittens all the time, she'll be a lot less thin and worried, poor thing. So they'll bring her back and she can live in the yard. We'll put scraps out for her."

"Thank you!" Alicia forgot to be shy and gave Emma a hug. "You're amazing. I never even thought of doing that!"

"Can we bring Catkin back to visit her?" Will asked, reaching into his bag and picking the sprinkles off his cupcake.

"Maybe." Alicia smiled, imagining the two cats nose to nose, sniffing hello. All of a sudden, she couldn't wait to get home and see Catkin and show her to Sarah, too.

Her own kitten, not-so-secret anymore....

Sammy the Shy Kitten

Contents

For Daisy

Chapter One
An Exciting Day

"See you later, Mom!" Emma waved as her mom drove off down the bumpy road that led to Cloverview Stables. She was looking forward to seeing her best friend Keira, but she would see most of her riding-class friends at school on Monday. Really she wanted to say hello to the ponies, and the cats that lived at the stables, too.

Emma didn't always see the cats—they were all very shy, almost wild. She wasn't even sure how many of them there were; no one was. Liz, who owned the riding school, said she thought there were five. But Emma was almost certain there were six, and that the skinny orange cat was actually two skinny orange cats. Once she thought she'd seen him strolling along the roof of the feed store only seconds after he'd been sunbathing out by the paddock.

Liz put out food and water for the cats, but only once a day. Mostly they lived by hunting. They earned their keep by getting rid of the mice and rats that sniffed around the stables looking for the horses' feed.

"Hello, Sparky," Emma said, going

to pat the nose of the gray she usually rode in her class. The pony snorted and put his nose over the half-door of his stall. He nudged happily at her hand, searching for an apple or a carrot. He knew Emma always brought him treats. Emma giggled and brought out a piece of carrot. "And I've got mints for afterward, if you're good," she whispered. "But don't tell the others. I'll just go and let Liz know I'm here, then I'll be back to tack you up."

Emma looked around hopefully for the cats as she went over to find Liz, but none of them seemed to be around. She crouched down and peeked behind the tulips in the little flowerbed in front of the office. The orange cat (one of the orange cats, anyway) practically lived in the flowerbed, and sometimes he'd let her pet him. Sure enough, there he was, curled up tightly into a striped ball. He opened one yellow-green eye and glared at her. He obviously didn't want to be petted.

Emma sighed and put her head around the office door.

"Hi, Liz. Mom dropped me off a little early so I could say hello to the ponies. I wanted to see if I could pet Midnight, too, but I can't find her."

Midnight was Emma's favorite of the stable cats—she was black and had longer fur than the others, with a thick bushy tail. She spent a lot of time lying in the sun and grooming, cleaning pieces of hay out of her pretty fur.

Liz had looked up, smiling, when she first spotted Emma, but now her smile faded. "I haven't actually seen her for a couple of days. I'm starting to get a little worried. I know the cats aren't really pets and they wander around all over the place, but usually Midnight's the friendliest of them all. She doesn't disappear like Coral and Candy, and she's almost always in the yard."

Emma nodded, frowning. "I don't think I've ever been to the stables and not seen her."

"She's been so hungry lately, but she hasn't come to the food bowls," Liz sighed. "I'm sure I'd have noticed her."

Emma glanced out at the bowls. Liz kept them by the bench in the yard, which had a wooden canopy built over it. It meant that the food stayed dry and the nervous cats didn't have to go inside for it. Emma smiled as she saw Susie, a thin little tabby, slinking over to see if there was anything left. But then she turned back toward Liz.

"So … Midnight hasn't eaten anything for two days?" she asked anxiously.

Liz shook her head. "Not from here, I don't think. She's a good mouser, so maybe she's just been hunting more. I wish I'd seen her around, though."

Emma nibbled her bottom lip. "At least the stables are far from the main road," she said slowly. Her Aunt Grace's cat, Whiskers, had been hit by a car a couple of years ago and had broken his leg really badly. He was better now, but Aunt Grace didn't like him going around to the front of the house. She always tried to tempt him back inside if she saw him sitting on the front wall.

Liz smiled at her. "Exactly. I'm probably worrying over nothing."

She didn't make Emma feel much

better, though. Where could Midnight have gone?

"Anyway," Liz said briskly. "We should get going. The others will be here by now." She got up and put an arm around Emma's shoulders. "Don't worry. You know what cats are like—especially these half-wild ones. We'll get all upset, and then she'll stroll in without a care in the world."

Emma giggled. But she wished that Midnight would stroll in now.

Maybe it was because she was thinking about Midnight, or maybe it was just a bad day, but nothing seemed to go right for Emma that morning. Tacking up Sparky took forever. He wouldn't stay still—he jittered and sidestepped and nibbled at her jacket. Then he almost stepped on her foot as she led him over to the outdoor arena.

"Are you okay?" her friend Keira asked as she finally managed to get to the gate. "You look a little stressed."

"Sparky's just being ... Sparky," Emma sighed. "He's wonderful when he wants to be, but...."

Keira grinned and nodded. "I know. Maybe he's just excited."

"He's always excited!"

"Are you ready, girls?" Liz came over to check that their girths were tight. "Now, the jumps are a little higher than last week, but you're all perfectly capable of clearing these fences. Just don't let the ponies try to take them too fast."

Emma nodded a little nervously. She really did love Sparky. The gentler ponies, like Keira's mount Jasmine, just didn't have as much personality as the bouncy gray. But she had a feeling that trying to keep Sparky calm and collected wouldn't be that easy today. Luckily, they were going first so Sparky wouldn't get bored. The thrill of riding a fast, eager pony took over as they set off, and Emma had a huge smile on her face by the time they'd cleared the second jump.

Then somehow everything went wrong. Maybe Sparky decided that he didn't like the look of the new rainbow-striped rails that Liz had used for the third jump. He slid around to the left of the jump instead of going over. Emma did her best to encourage him, but Sparky was determined—he swerved sideways around the jump, and Emma felt herself slipping out of the saddle. There was a horrible, slow moment when she knew she was falling. Then all of a sudden she was on the ground, with her ankle twisted and aching, and Sparky standing over her. He looked very apologetic.

"Emma!" Liz came hurrying over, catching Sparky's reins and handing them to Keira. "Hold on to him, Keira, while I check that Emma's all right."

"I don't think I rode him at it straight enough," Emma said, wincing as she tried to stand. "Ow, my ankle...."

Liz gently felt the ankle through Emma's boot. "I don't think it's swelling up. Do you want me to call Alex and get him to bring you an ice pack?"

"It's okay. Sorry I messed up...."

"No, you were doing really well. It looked like Sparky just decided against that jump. Can you put any weight on your ankle?"

"I think so." Emma blinked, trying not to cry.

Liz helped her up. "Are you sure you're all right?"

Emma nodded. "It was just a shock...."

"Here, sit down on the bench. We'll tie Sparky up to the fence, and I'll come and check on you again in a little while."

Liz went back to schooling the others over the jumps, and Emma watched from the side of the arena, gently rubbing her ankle. It was starting to feel a little better already. She clapped as Keira jumped Jasmine clear, and her friend waved at her.

Emma stood up and leaned on the fence, testing the weight on her ankle. It was definitely feeling better. She was just thinking about asking Liz if it was okay to untie Sparky again when she heard a strange squeaky noise behind her. She glanced around. The outdoor arena was next to a shabby old barn that Liz was planning to get rid of so they could make the arena bigger. It was divided up into stalls for horses, but they weren't used anymore. The noise was definitely coming from in there, though. Emma limped curiously over to the door—that was falling apart, too; a couple of the boards had rotted away at the bottom.

She lifted the latch, pushed open the door, and looked around it cautiously. Maybe a bird had gotten trapped inside—she didn't like the idea of it flapping out at her. But there was no bird, only the raspy creak of the door—and then that tiny, breathy little squeak again. Emma walked in slowly, following the noise. It sounded like it was coming from the stall at the end.

Emma stopped and peered around the open half-door. There was still some straw on the floor, piled up in the corner. The squeaking was coming from over there, and for one horrible moment, Emma wondered if it was a rat.

Then a dark head looked up over the straw, and Emma laughed in surprise.

"Midnight!" she said, keeping her voice low. "Liz is really worried about you, you know. What are you doing in here?"

Midnight eyed her cautiously, her ears flickering, and Emma frowned. She'd never heard Midnight squeak like that before, she realized. And there was something else in the straw—something small and wriggly and dark. Actually, there were several somethings....

"Oh! Midnight, did you...?" Emma stepped closer, trying to lean over the door just a little so she could see without scaring the cat. She'd completely forgotten about her twisted ankle now. "You did! You had kittens!"

Chapter Two
The Discovery

The kittens were so sweet, squirming around over each other in the straw and nuzzling at their mother. Midnight glared suspiciously at Emma for a moment. Then she obviously decided that it was safe to ignore her and went back to licking her babies all over. Emma tried not to giggle. It looked as though Midnight was determined that they would be just as beautifully groomed as she was.

"So that's why you were really hungry. It's okay, Midnight. I won't come any closer." Emma hung on to the doorjamb, counting. "It's three, isn't it?" she whispered. "Two black kittens and one gray tabby. I should go and tell the others...." But she didn't want to leave just yet. The kittens were so little. Emma wondered when they'd been born.

"I'd better go and tell Liz," she said at last, slowly backing away. "Don't go anywhere, okay?" She had read about mother cats picking up their kittens in their mouths to move them if they thought they weren't safe. She hoped she hadn't scared Midnight into doing anything like that. But Midnight didn't look too worried. "I'll get Liz to find you some food, too," Emma added, her eyes widening. "Oh, Midnight, you must be starving!"

As soon as she was out of sight of Midnight, Emma twirled around and limped out of the barn as fast as she could.

Liz waved when she saw her and hurried over. "Emma! I just noticed that you'd disappeared. How's your ankle? It doesn't look like it's swollen."

Emma shook her head, grinning at Liz. "No, it feels a lot better now. And I found Midnight."

"Oh, that's great! Where was she? Is she all right?"

Emma giggled. "She's more than all

right. You have to come and see!"

"I need to watch the others. Can you show me at the end of class?" Liz glanced between Emma and the rest of the girls, and Emma realized that of course she couldn't leave them riding without an instructor.

"It's okay. I don't think Midnight's going anywhere." Emma folded her arms and glanced back at the barn.

Liz sighed. "I hope this is worth all the suspense, Emma! Come on, you'd better catch up with the others. Sparky looks like he's feeling left out."

Sparky did seem to think that he'd been missing out. He brightened up when he saw Emma and jumped two clear rounds with her as soon as he was allowed back into the ring.

"You rascal!" Emma told him affectionately as she patted his nose afterward. "You can have a treat— here. But I don't think you deserve it. Why didn't you do that the first time around, instead of tossing me off?" Sparky gobbled up the treat from her hand eagerly, and Emma smiled. "I guess if I hadn't fallen, I wouldn't have found the kittens. Oh, look, Liz is waving. It's the end of the lesson now—I can't wait for her to see them." She hugged Sparky around the neck and started to walk him back to the gate where the others were waiting. "I'm not showing you, though. I wouldn't trust you not to put your huge, clumpy feet on those kittens."

"What are you so excited about?" Keira asked as she led Jasmine over toward Emma and Sparky.

"I found Midnight! Liz hadn't seen her for a couple of days, and she was getting worried. You have to come and see!"

Keira looked at her doubtfully. "I'm sorry, Emma. You know I'm scared of cats."

"I forgot! I'm sorry, I was just so excited." She bit her lip, not wanting Keira to miss out on the secret. But she knew her friend was especially frightened of the half-wild cats at the stables. She leaned over to whisper in Keira's ear. "Midnight had kittens. In the old barn! Don't tell Liz, yet, okay?"

Keira smiled. "Now I understand why you're so excited. Are they cute?" She sounded a little wistful, as though she wished she wasn't so nervous around cats.

"I only saw them from a distance, but they were beautiful. Are you sure you don't want just a quick look?"

Keira shook her head. "Midnight's so jumpy...."

Liz came up behind them. "Are you going to show me this big secret now?"

Emma nodded eagerly, and Keira laughed. "She can't wait. I'm surprised she hasn't told everybody already! Here, I'll lead Sparky back."

Emma handed over the reins and hurried Liz along to the barn door. "Be really quiet!" she whispered, putting a finger up to her lips. Then she led the way inside, tiptoeing over the dusty floor.

"Where is she?" Liz whispered, and then she gasped as Emma pulled her sleeve and pointed into the stall. "Kittens! Oh, wow, I never even thought of that!"

"Three of them," Emma said, beaming. "Aren't they beautiful? Can we put some food for Midnight in here? I bet she's really hungry."

Liz nodded. "Yes, definitely. I'll go and get her some now. Gosh, three more cats. That's a lot...."

Emma looked up at her worriedly. "I hadn't thought about that."

Liz made a face. "Well, they are beautiful, but I'm not sure how many more cats we can take care of, to be honest. We've already got five. I suppose I should have expected this to happen, but none of them have had kittens until now. Probably we should have gotten them spayed or neutered, but they're all so shy. It was a nightmare the one time I had to take Coral to the vet because she'd been in a fight. She was really tricky to catch, and she hated being in the car."

"So...." Emma swallowed—her

mouth had gone dry with excitement. When she spoke again, her voice sounded oddly squeaky. "If the kittens couldn't stay here, would you want to find homes for them?"

Liz nodded slowly. "That would be perfect, wouldn't it? Nice homes where they'd be taken care of and loved."

Emma gazed thoughtfully at the wriggling bundles of fur. "I didn't think of them being pets," she replied. "I thought they'd be a little wild, like Midnight."

Liz shook her head. "I think it has to do with how much they get used to people when they're little. Midnight and Susie and the others are half-wild because they've never had a real indoor home or spent much time around people. But it doesn't mean it has to be the same with these little ones."

Emma nodded. That made sense. "How are you going to find homes for them?" she asked. "Would you just ... ask people if they wanted them?"

Liz smiled at Emma. "I suppose so. Are you thinking you'd like a kitten? What would your mom and dad say?"

"I don't know." Emma sighed. "But I can ask. I love the idea of taming a little wild kitten!"

Liz snorted. "I wouldn't put it that way to your mom, Emma. She'd worry about you getting your fingers bitten off. Come on, let's go and find Midnight something to eat."

Chapter Three
Emma's Plan

"Dad!" Emma ran over to the car where her dad was waiting and flung her arms around his waist. "You'll never guess what happened!"

Her dad blinked at her in surprise. "Did Sparky behave himself for once?"

Emma shook her head and laughed. "Nope, actually he was really naughty, and I fell off. But I'm okay! It's

Midnight—she's had three kittens, and I found them!"

"That is exciting! Are they really small?"

"I think they're only a day or two old," Emma explained. "Liz said Midnight had disappeared for a couple of days, so I guess she went off to hide and make herself a little nest. The kittens are tiny—only about this big." She held her hands apart to show him. "Do you want to come and see?"

Dad wrinkled his nose. "I'd love to—but what about Midnight? Isn't she really shy? If a lot of people start trampling past her kittens, she might get upset."

Emma nodded. "I know. But Liz said that since I found them, I can take some food back for Midnight. You could come with me. Liz even made her a special treat—she found some fish in the freezer. She figures Midnight deserves it!"

Dad grinned. "I haven't seen any tiny kittens in years—not since my cat Bella had kittens when I was about your age."

"Did she?" Emma looked surprised. "Didn't you have her spayed, then?"

"She was a stray that Grandma May

adopted," Dad explained. "Well, she adopted us, really. She was sitting on the front doorstep one day when we came home from school. We hadn't even gotten as far as taking her to the vet, to be honest. We were just getting used to having a cat when the kittens arrived. We had her spayed after that.... One litter of kittens was fun, but your grandma didn't want to find homes for any more."

"You're so lucky," Emma sighed. "I wish we had kittens. Or a grown-up cat—I wouldn't mind." She gave her dad a sideways look. "Dad, if you really like cats, why don't we have one?"

Her dad looked thoughtful. "Well, it would have been tricky when Mom and I were both working full-time. But

I suppose now that we've changed our shifts around we could...." Emma's parents both worked at the local hospital. "I don't know what your mom would think, though, Ems. She's never had a cat."

"I don't see how anybody could not like a tiny little kitten," Emma said coaxingly.

"Maybe because it'll turn into a great big cat clawing the couch? You know your mom likes everything really clean and neat in the house."

"A cat could be clean and neat...," Emma said hopefully. "Oh, look! Liz has the food!" Liz was standing by the parking lot gate, holding a couple of bowls. Emma grabbed her dad's arm, hauling him after her.

"We'll be really careful," she told Liz as she took the food bowl. "Oh, you brought some water, too. I was going to ask you about that."

Emma's dad took the water bowl and followed Emma across the yard to the old barn. "I can hear them rustling around," he whispered to Emma as they tiptoed over to the stall.

Midnight was looking anxious, and

she half stood up as Emma and her dad came to the door of the stall. The kittens squeaked a little and shifted around in the straw nest as their mother moved. Emma ducked her head, trying to see the kittens without staring at Midnight— she knew from a cat program she'd seen on TV that cats didn't like to make eye contact sometimes. "It's okay," she whispered. "We brought you some yummy food. Fish—can you smell it?"

She was sure that Midnight's whiskers flickered, and the fluffy cat was definitely eyeing the bowls.

"I'll put the food here." Emma crouched down and stretched out her arm, trying to get the bowl into the stall without scaring Midnight. "And Dad has some water for you, too." She glanced across at her dad. "Can you see the kittens? Look, they don't even have their eyes open yet!"

The kittens wriggled and made tiny meowing noises, calling for Midnight to feed them. They were like little furry balloons, Emma thought, all plump and squishy. Their fur was still short and fine, so the pink skin showed through on their tummies and paws, and their tails were almost as thin as string.

"I wish we could stay and watch," she whispered to Dad as she edged away, still crouching. "But Midnight might not want to eat while we're here because it'll mean leaving the kittens."

"I know. She is looking a little worried," Dad agreed. "I love that little tabby. It looks like it's going to have beautiful silver and black stripes. But they're all cute."

"I like that one, too," Emma whispered, giving the kittens one last look from the doorway. "That's the kind of cat I've always imagined having."

Snuggled in the straw, the kittens meowed faintly and stumbled their way over toward their mother and her milk. They were so little that food and warmth were the only things they understood. They heard the soft vibrations of Emma's voice, and her dad's, but only Midnight understood that Emma had brought food and water and had kept her distance from the precious kittens.

"The kitten of one of those cats at the stables?" Emma's mom asked doubtfully. "I don't think that's a very good idea, Emma. I know they look beautiful, but none of them is friendly. They're all half-wild. I don't think we want a cat like that." She put the salad on the kitchen table and sat down. "It isn't that I don't want us to have a pet, but we've never had a cat before. Shouldn't

177

it be somebody who really knows what they're doing taking care of kittens like those?"

"But there isn't anybody who knows!" Emma tried to argue. "Liz would be really happy if we wanted to adopt one. I know she would. You should see him, Mom, the little gray tabby kitten. He has white paws and white under his chin. His nose is all pink and soft because he's so small."

Mom smiled at her. "He sounds beautiful, Emma. But a kitten like that might be a lot of work. Maybe we could find one from somewhere else."

Emma looked desperately at her dad. She should be delighted—Mom had never said anything about being able to get a cat before. Emma knew that she was lucky to have her riding lessons—she'd never thought they'd be able to have a pet at home, too. But now she didn't want just any cat; she wanted to help those little kittens at the stables.

She'd always felt sorry for the stable cats, not having real homes to go to. They didn't seem to mind—they curled up together in the stalls, and Liz put food out for them—but it wasn't like a cozy, warm basket by the radiator, or sleeping at the foot of someone's bed. She didn't want the kittens to grow up wild like their mother, even though Midnight was beautiful.

"Let's see what we can find out about taming kittens," Dad suggested. "They were very sweet. And I think it's too late to turn Emma off of them. She's already fallen in love with the little tabby. Do you think it's a boy or a girl? We didn't get close enough to check."

"I thought he was a boy, just because he looked like he was wearing a little white shirt. But I don't know for sure."

Emma's dad looked over at her mom, and she smiled.

"We'll see," Mom said. "I'm not promising anything, but maybe you could do some research. Find out what we'd have to do…."

"Yes!" Emma squealed. "Oh, Mom, this is so exciting! Please can we hurry up and eat lunch so I can look it all up on the computer?"

"Hello, Cloverview Stables?"

"Hi, Liz," Emma said, a bit shyly. She'd never called the stables before. Usually Mom did it if they had to book a lesson.

"Oh! Is that you, Emma? Is everything okay? How's your ankle?"

"It doesn't hurt at all now. I'm just calling because I've been talking to Mom and Dad about the kittens. I asked if we could adopt one, but my mom's not sure. She says maybe it should be somebody who's more experienced with cats." Emma frowned to herself, trying to remember all the information that she and Dad had looked up that afternoon. "But the thing is, if they're going to be adopted, the kittens need to have a lot of contact with people so they're not shy around humans like Midnight and the others are. So I was wondering if I could come and spend some time with them."

"Yes, that makes sense," Liz said slowly. "And it's wonderful that you want to help take care of them, Emma. Of course you can, if your mom and dad are fine with it."

"Oh, they are," Emma told her. She hesitated, and then went on, "I'm really hoping Mom will let me adopt one of the kittens, if I can help tame them. At the moment, she's worried that they'll be too wild. But we've found a ton of ways to help with that. Dad and I have been doing a lot of research. It's the little tabby one I really love."

"He's adorable, isn't he? So, is there anything I should be doing? Or the others at the stables?" Liz asked.

"I think just try to spend some time with them. Would it be okay if I came to the stables after school sometimes, as well as for my lessons? The more the kittens get used to people, the better. I'm guessing you want to find homes for the others, too?"

Emma heard Liz sigh on the phone. "Yes, I need to think about that. Maybe I'll put a flyer up on the board outside the stables."

"Oh!" Emma suddenly remembered something she'd read on a website.

"There's a charity that will help with spaying and neutering the cats. They'll even come and get them for you! They'll catch them and neuter them for free, and then bring them back."

"Really? That sounds amazing. Could you find their details for me, please?" Liz laughed. "You really are serious about cats, aren't you, Emma?"

Chapter Four
A Perfect Day

Emma went to the stables whenever she could get Mom or Dad to drive her. She spent most of her allowance on a cat care book, just in case she did manage to persuade Mom to take the tabby kitten home. The kitten wouldn't be allowed to leave his mother until he was seven or eight weeks old, anyway. They had to give the kittens the chance to learn everything they needed to know from Midnight. So Emma had plenty of time to read the whole book and persuade her mom that the tabby kitten would be the perfect pet.

The first time she went, Emma just sat quietly by the door. Midnight watched her suspiciously, her ears laid back and the tip of her fluffy tail twitching. It was obvious to Emma that she was making Midnight nervous, but she had to get to know the kittens. It was so important. She wrapped her arms around her knees and just sat listening to the squeaks and rustles in the straw. By the time Dad came to pick her up, Midnight was lying down feeding the kittens as if Emma wasn't there.

On her next visit, Emma decided to bring Midnight some cat treats. If Midnight was distracted, she might let Emma near the kittens. Liz had told her that Midnight had licked the bowl of fish spotlessly clean, so Emma decided to get fish-flavored ones.

She crouched down not too far from the kittens and shook some treats out of the packet next to Midnight. The cat sniffed at them curiously. Emma could tell she wanted the fishy treats, but that she wasn't ready to eat in front of her. Emma sat with her chin on her knees, looking away from Midnight. Out of the corner of her eye, she could just see Midnight edging closer to the pile.

Midnight made one last little hop and started to gobble down the treats. Then she sniffed cautiously at Emma's right foot—the part of her that was closest— and darted back to her kittens. Emma couldn't stop herself from beaming. It felt like a breakthrough.

She opened the packet again, making sure that Midnight could hear it rustle. Then she wriggled a little closer, shaking out a few more treats right next to the cat. Emma really wanted to get a good look at the kittens, as she thought they must be about a week old by now. She was hoping that their eyes would be open. Her cat book said that the kittens would all have blue eyes to begin with.

"They're definitely bigger," Emma whispered to Midnight, who was still eating the treats. "They're beautiful." Midnight looked up at Emma with her ears laid back, and Emma sighed. "I know you don't like me talking. I don't want to scare you. I just want them to get used to hearing my voice. Anybody's voice, really."

Midnight crunched the last fishy treat, and Emma took a deep breath. She had petted the cat a couple of times before, but not since she'd had the kittens. Slowly, she held out her hand to let Midnight sniff it.

Midnight nudged her nose at Emma's

hand cautiously, but she didn't hiss or raise the fur on her back. She actually looked calm. She rubbed her chin along Emma's wrist, and then strolled back toward the kittens.

Emma held her breath and put the same hand down in the straw, next to the kittens. Midnight lay down, stretched out beside her babies, and Emma smiled delightedly. She was almost touching them! And the little tabby was right next to her hand. Emma wondered if he could smell the fishy treats, too, but she thought he was probably too young for that. His eyes were definitely open, though—just tiny blue slits. He looked like a teddy bear, with his round face and little triangle ears.

"I'm so lucky," Emma whispered, "getting to know you now when you're so small."

The kitten meowed squeakily and waved his front paws, wriggling closer to Emma. "I'm not your mom, little one," she whispered. "I think you want to be over there. For some milk." Very gently she scooped him closer to Midnight so he could latch on and suckle. His fur was the softest thing she'd ever felt.

"I've got to think of a name," Emma muttered. "I can't just keep calling you little one. Sam maybe? Or Sammy…. You look like a Sammy. My little Sammy cat."

As the weeks went by, Sammy and the other kittens grew amazingly quickly. By four weeks they could all walk properly, and suddenly they seemed to be interested in everything.

Midnight spent a lot of her time trying to herd them back together, hurrying around them in the scattered straw and shooing them back to the nest. But as soon as she had one kitten safely tucked away, the other two would be padding out to explore again. Emma thought that Midnight looked very tired. Liz had been putting down a lot more food for her than usual, and Emma had been bringing her bowls of special cat milk and extra snacks, but it was hard work herding kittens and feeding them, too.

The kittens were more like mini cats now—their heads still seemed much too big for their little bodies, but they'd lost their furry balloon look. They were really growing up.

"Hello," Emma whispered, crouching down by the door of the stall. Three little heads popped up at once, and she giggled. They looked so funny, like the meerkats she'd seen at the zoo. Almost at once the tabby kitten plunged over the edge of the straw nest to come and see her.

"I've got something really special for you," Emma said. She and Liz had been talking about how they were going to wean the kittens—to get them eating food as well as Midnight's milk. Emma had looked it up in her book, and Mom had bought some baby rice and evaporated milk from the supermarket to mix up for the kittens. It looked disgusting, but then Emma didn't much like the look of regular cat food, either.

She'd bought a special litter box as well to put in the corner of the stall. According to her book, now that the kittens were trying solid food, they were going to poop a lot more, too. Until now, Liz had just scooped out the dirty straw every day.

Liz had said that she'd be able to do

most of the feedings and cleaning, and Alex and Sarah, who also taught at the stables, had said they could help, too. The kittens were going to need to eat four times a day, so it was lucky Liz and the others were around.

"This is going to be yummy," Emma promised, dipping her finger in the white goo and holding it out to Sammy.

Sammy sniffed curiously, and Emma rubbed the goo on his nose. He stepped back in surprise and sneezed. Then he licked at the dribbles of baby rice that were running down his muzzle. It was good! He licked harder, running his bright pink tongue all around his mouth and nose.

Sammy padded closer to the girl, hoping for more of the white stuff. Emma was holding some out for him, and he licked it right off her finger this time, trying to gobble it up fast. He could hear his brother and sister coming up behind him, and he didn't want to share.

"Look," Emma whispered. "There's a whole bowlful...."

Sammy sniffed hopefully at the bowl, and then started to lap hurriedly. The other two kittens appeared beside him, and his sister plunged her face into the bowl eagerly. She came up smeared in white milky stuff, dripping from her nose and her black whiskers.

The girl laughed, and all the kittens jumped, staring at her nervously.

"I'm sorry," she whispered softly.

Sammy watched her for a moment, then decided that she didn't mean any harm and went back to lapping. The food was so tasty, but it was making him sleepy, just like feeding from his mother did sometimes. He licked at the last smears at the bottom of the bowl, and then licked his whiskers and yawned.

His brother and sister began to pad back toward their mother, to sleep curled up next to her, but the nest in the straw was a long way away. Sammy yawned again and eyed the girl. She was warm, too—he knew it from the times she'd petted him. He walked toward her, wobbling a little, and tried to climb up her leg.

Emma looked at him, smiling in delighted surprise. Then she gently scooped a hand underneath his bottom and lifted him up onto her lap. Sammy flopped down, full and sleepy, and began a tiny purr.

"Oh, Emma," Mom whispered from the doorway. "Is that Sammy? You said it was the tabby one you really liked."

"Yes," Emma breathed. "He fell asleep on me. And he was purring, Mom."

"He is beautiful," Mom said, smiling. "What does Midnight think about him sleeping on you?"

Emma giggled. "She's asleep, too. I think she's grateful! She must be worn out taking care of them all. I need to ask Liz if she has something we can put across the doorway of the stall, a plank of wood maybe. So that Midnight can get out, but the kittens won't. Otherwise they'll be wandering all over the place soon. We might never find them!" She sighed. "I guess we have to go, don't we?"

"We can stay for a little longer. I don't want to make you move him. Why don't I go and ask Liz about finding something for the door?"

Emma nodded. Then, as her mom was turning to leave, she suddenly whispered, "Mom!"

"What is it? Is he waking up after all?"

"No, it's just … do you think we could adopt him? You said we had to see about having one of Midnight's kittens—in case they were too wild."

Her mom looked down at Sammy, stretched out blissfully on Emma's knee. "He doesn't look very wild, does he?"

Emma shook her head, beaming.

Mom smiled at her. "All right, we can adopt him. I'll tell Liz now."

Chapter Five
Going Home

Keira stood by the door of the stall, looking cautiously around it at Midnight and the dancing kittens. Emma had managed to persuade her to come and see them at last. They were playing with a toy that Emma had bought—a bundle of feathers on the end of a long wire that she could flick and wave around. The kittens loved it.

They stalked it, pounced on it, bounced around it, and all the while Midnight sat watching them proudly. Every so often she couldn't resist and put out a paw to dab at the feathers, too.

"They're so funny," Keira whispered to Emma. "I wish…."

"You could take a turn," Emma suggested, holding out the toy.

Keira shook her head. "No," she said quickly. "It's okay."

Emma wanted to persuade her, but she had a feeling it would only make Keira feel worse. "I want to wear Sammy out a little, before Dad comes and we put him in the cat carrier," she explained. Dad was bringing the carrier when he came to pick Emma up from her lesson, anytime now.

"Do you think Sammy won't like it?" Keira asked.

"I don't know." Emma sighed. "It feels mean taking him away from Midnight and the other kittens, but he's about nine weeks old. A lot of kittens go to new homes then, even though it's a little early. From the websites Dad and I looked at, it sounded like it'd be best to adopt Sammy as soon as possible. Otherwise, he'll do whatever his mom does. Midnight still doesn't really like being touched, and she'd never let me pick her up. I don't want Sammy to learn to be scared of people from her."

"What's going to happen to the other kittens?" Keira asked.

"Liz thinks she's found a lady who wants them," Emma said happily. "She's had cats before, and she's going to take them both together. Later this week, I think." She glanced anxiously at Midnight, who was still watching her kittens closely. "Poor Midnight. She'll really miss them. But it's the best thing for the kittens, I'm sure."

"Oh! Your dad's here," Keira said, turning to look out the barn door.

Emma let out an excited gasp. "Oh, wow...," she said. "I'm actually getting to take you home, Sammy!"

She had brought along a packet of cat treats so they could tempt Sammy into the carrier. The kittens were eating dry food like Midnight now, although theirs was made for kittens. The cat treats were a special extra. Emma took the carrier from her dad and opened the wire door. Then she scattered a few treats inside. Midnight and all the kittens edged closer—they knew what that rustling noise meant.

"They're all coming," Emma said worriedly to Dad.

"That's probably not a bad thing. We want Sammy to think the box isn't scary. If they all play around in it for a while, he won't mind going in, will he?"

"I guess not." Emma watched as all three kittens explored their way around the carrier, nibbling at the treats and sniffing the soft cushion lining. Even Midnight snapped up a treat that was just by the door.

"Emma, look," Dad whispered, a few minutes later. "Sammy's going in on his own. You can close the door in a second."

Emma nodded, and as the white tip of Sammy's striped tail cleared the door, she gently swung it shut and twisted the latches.

"Let's go home," she whispered.

Sammy sat pressed against the back of the box. He had no idea what was happening—he'd never seen anything but the barn. Now he was shut into the small, shadowy carrier, and somehow it was moving. The smells were strange and sharp, and there was so much noise. The vibration of the car was completely new to Sammy and very scary.

He could hear Emma's voice, and her dad's, and he knew that they were familiar, but it wasn't making him feel much better.

"Do you think he's all right? I thought he might meow, but he's not even making any noise."

"It's a big shock for him, poor kitten. We're almost home, Emma."

"We're almost home," Emma repeated, whispering through the holes in the carrier. "Not much longer."

Sammy felt himself pressed against the side of the carrier as the car swung around a corner. He let out a little hiss of fright and tried to back farther into the box—but there wasn't anywhere to go. He scratched at the plastic, just a faint little movement of his paw. Nothing happened. Sammy closed his eyes and hoped his mother would come.

"I don't understand," Emma whispered. "He was so friendly before. He let me pick him up. He even slept on my lap."

"One of those websites did say to expect a kitten to take a couple of steps backward when it's moved, Ems," Dad pointed out. "He's only been here a few hours."

"I didn't think he'd be this jumpy." Mom looked worriedly at Sammy, tense and nervous, his whiskers bristling.

"He's just scared," Dad said encouragingly.

"I guess so…," Mom sighed.

Emma looked over at the big wire crate they'd borrowed from one of the neighbors, whose puppy didn't need it anymore. Sammy couldn't be loose in the house just yet, as he'd probably run off and hide. But they could put the crate on the table in the corner of the kitchen, and he could see everything that was going on and get used to a lot of people being around. The kitchen didn't have any holes a kitten could get stuck in when they let him out to play.

It had seemed like the perfect plan for an almost-wild kitten. But Emma had imagined Sammy watching curiously as she ate her breakfast or did her homework. She'd thought of him purring to Dad as he made dinner. She hadn't seen a hissing, spitting, miserable little kitten hiding at the back of his crate. He'd even swiped at her with his claws when she put a bowl of fresh water in for him. He'd missed, but still. It was like Sammy was a different kitten.

"We need to give him time," Dad said gently. "A day or so to calm down before we start trying to handle him again."

"Yes," Emma sighed. "And I know I should have expected that he wouldn't be very happy...." But she hadn't thought it would be like this. Mom looked so worried—and she'd really been warming up to the idea of a kitten! What if she changed her mind?

Dad patted Emma's shoulder, and then gave Mom a hug. "Don't look so tragic, you two! It'll be okay! I'm going to make some coffee. Do you want anything, Emma?"

Emma shook her head. Deep down, she realized sadly, she'd just thought that Sammy would see how nice their house was. He'd know how excited she was to have a kitten of her own— he'd understand, and he'd settle in right away.

"I was being silly," Emma muttered to herself. She crouched down in front of the crate, looking at Sammy sideways. He was still huddled in the back, his ears flat against his little head. "I thought everything would be perfect all at once. But I'll do anything to make you love us, Sammy. I just want you to be happy."

Chapter Six
Settling In

Emma held out her fingers to Sammy. They were covered in roast chicken dinner baby food, which apparently was the most popular flavor with kittens. It felt sticky and gloppy, but she didn't mind. They'd given Sammy an entire 24 hours to calm down, and Emma just couldn't wait anymore. All the websites said that the way to make a half-wild kitten like you was to use food. They had to make Sammy see that food came from people, and if he wanted the food, he had to put up with them, too.

"He noticed, Ems," Dad breathed behind her. "He can smell it."

It was true. Emma could see Sammy's ears flicking, just a little. And his eyes were widening. "He must be able to smell it," she said. "It smells disgusting."

"Not to a cat," Dad whispered back.

"He's coming!" Emma tried not to sound too excited, or too loud. Sammy was stepping delicately, cautiously across the crate to sniff at her fingers. His tiny pink tongue flicked out, and he began to lick them.

Emma kept a straight face, trying

not to laugh and scare him away, but it tickled so much. His tongue was very strong for such a small kitten. And it was so rough. Emma leaned a little closer so she could see the tiny white hairs all over his tongue. Sammy stopped licking and glanced worriedly up at her for a second. But then the deliciousness of the baby food won, and he went back to getting every last bit out from under Emma's fingernails.

Emma wanted to pull her hand away to get some more from the jar, but she was sure that would frighten Sammy. Then she rolled her eyes. Of course! She dipped her other hand in, lifting out several fingerfuls, and slowly moved that hand into the crate, too.

Sammy moved his head from side to side, as though he wasn't sure which hand to go for.

"Aww, poor Sammy—you've confused him now," Dad said.

Sammy decided that he couldn't get much more from Emma's right hand and changed to gulping down the food from her left. Emma looked at him thoughtfully. Her right hand was still in the crate. Very gently, she ran her hand down Sammy's back. He tensed a little, but he didn't spring away. Emma kept softly petting his fur.

"Is that nice?" she whispered. "Is it nice being petted?"

Sammy glanced up at her, as if to check what the noise was, but he kept licking.

"Keep petting him," Dad whispered. "I'm going to get a little bowl of his dry food. Let's see if we can get him to eat that with us still here watching him."

He filled the bowl quietly and passed it to Emma so she could put it in front of Sammy. The little kitten darted back as the bowl suddenly appeared, but then he caught the scent of the dry cat food he was used to. He gave Emma's fingers one last hopeful swipe with his tongue and moved on to the bowl.

"You try petting him," Emma whispered to Dad.

Dad nodded and reached slowly into the crate, running one finger down Sammy's back as he busily gobbled the food. Sammy glanced over his shoulder, but he didn't stop eating.

"It really works," Dad said. "We can do this again when we feed him at lunchtime."

Emma nodded. "Every time we feed him. And maybe soon we can get him out of the crate and let him eat from his bowl on the floor." She sighed happily. "It's really going to be okay, Dad. I'm sure it is."

"Which top do you think I should wear?" Mom held two out on hangers.

"Hmm. The black one," Emma said, watching Sammy. He had almost finished his bowl of food and was looking sleepy. She had her arm inside his cage, with her hand cupped around him. Emma had a feeling he might fall asleep with her hand still there, which would be wonderful. He'd be almost back to the same friendly Sammy she'd known at the stables, and it was only a week since they'd brought him home.

"Are you sure?" Mom frowned. "You didn't look for very long...."

"Yes, Mom. I can pet Sammy and look, you know. Hurry up! Aunt Grace will be here to babysit soon."

Mom rushed off, and Emma giggled and gently moved the food bowl. Sammy had fallen asleep with his head in it! He twitched a little and then flopped down, collapsing across her hand with a little wheezy snore. She leaned against the crate, closing her eyes and smiling dreamily to herself. Soon they'd be able to take him out of there and he'd be a real pet. She was sure of it.

"Are you asleep, Emma?"

"Oh! Aunt Grace. I'm not, but Sammy is." Emma reached out the arm that wasn't in the crate to hug her aunt. "I didn't hear you come in."

"Your dad was walking up the path when I pulled up so I didn't have to ring the bell. He just went to change his clothes. So this is Sammy? He's beautiful."

"Isn't he?" Emma agreed proudly. "And he's getting much more confident again. He was really upset on Saturday when we brought him home, but he's a lot happier now." Carefully, she slid her hand out from underneath him, and Sammy snuffled but stayed asleep. She grinned at her aunt. "My arm feels all prickly now! Mom asked if you could please help me with my science homework, and then she said we could watch a movie afterward."

Emma yawned and snuggled against Aunt Grace. "Can't we watch a little more?"

"No! You know your mom said eight-thirty, young lady. Besides, don't you have to feed Sammy before bed?"

"Oh, yes, and you haven't seen him awake yet! I forgot!" Emma sprang up from the couch. "I'll go and get his food." She hurried into the kitchen and began to measure it out, while Sammy padded up and down the crate, watching her and meowing hopefully.

Emma had just opened the door of the crate to put the bowl in when Aunt Grace pushed open the kitchen door. It banged slightly, and Sammy jumped at the noise. He saw Aunt Grace—someone he'd never met before—and suddenly panicked. He hissed loudly, and Emma stared at him. "What's the matter, Sammy?"

"Oh, dear, is he okay?" Aunt Grace asked, leaning over to look at him.

Sammy hissed again as he saw the strange person coming closer. He darted out of the crate door, desperate to get away.

"I think he's a little scared because you're new," Emma said worriedly, trying to catch him. "Maybe you'd better just let me calm him down, Aunt

Grace."

Aunt Grace stepped back out of the kitchen, but Sammy was already spooked. He scrambled over Emma's arm in a panic, accidentally clawing at her wrist so that she squeaked and dropped the food bowl.

The bowl smashed on the tiles with a huge crash, and Sammy yowled in fright. He raced around the side of the crate, but the table was pushed up against the wall below the window, and there was nowhere to go. Frantically, he clawed his way up the curtains, digging his tiny claws into the fabric.

Sammy hung there, swaying a little. He didn't really understand what had happened. He'd been about to eat his food—he could smell it—and then suddenly everything was different and terrifying. Now he didn't even know where he was, or how he'd gotten so high up.

The curtain fabric ripped a little under his weight, and he slid down a few inches with a frightened meow. He tried to claw his way back up again, but the shiny fabric was difficult to climb, and he slipped farther down.

"Sammy, it's all right...." Emma's voice, low and soothing. And now he wasn't falling anymore. Her hands were around him, the way they were when she fed him sometimes. After struggling for a moment, he let her unhook his paws from the few last threads of the curtains, and sat tensely in her hands, ears back and fur fluffed up. She brought him down, still whispering gently, and slid him back into the crate. Sammy backed away from the door anxiously, but the strange person was gone now, he could see. It was just Emma. He knew her. She was safe.

228

Chapter Seven
Trouble!

"Emma! You're still up!"

Emma jerked awake. Mom was standing in the living-room doorway, looking surprised.

"I'm sorry," said Aunt Grace. "Emma was upset, and I didn't want to make her go to bed...."

"What happened?" Dad asked, just at the same time as Mom noticed Emma's scratched wrist and swooped down to check it.

"Emma, you've hurt yourself! Oh, no, was it Sammy?"

"He didn't mean to." Emma looked sleepily at Dad and Mom. "It was an accident. And, um, I broke his food bowl. I'm sorry.... We swept it up."

"What's been going on?" Dad sat down on the arm of the couch, and Mom came to sit next to Emma.

Emma sighed. She was so tired that it was hard to explain. "I went to feed him, but he was scared of Aunt Grace."

"It was my fault. I should have thought, of course, he's never seen me before," Aunt Grace put in. "And he's more nervous than most kittens. I frightened him and he jumped out of the crate and scratched Emma by accident."

"And that made me drop his bowl, and he got even more scared and ran up the curtains."

"Oh my goodness," Mom muttered.

"I'm afraid he did tear them a little," Aunt Grace went on slowly. "But he's back in the crate now, and he's calmed down. In fact, the last time Emma checked, he was asleep, wasn't he?"

Emma nodded.

Mom leaned back against the couch and let out a huge sigh. "I knew this was a mistake. We should never have brought him home. He was so upset when we took him away from the stables and his mom. I just don't think it's fair."

"Mom!" Emma gasped.

"Oh, Emma. You have to see I'm right—just look at your wrist!"

Emma looked down at the three long red lines, and the little scratches that she'd gotten all over her hands when she was taking Sammy off the curtains. They were sore, but it hadn't been Sammy's fault. He was just scared—he hadn't meant to hurt her.

Mom put her arm around Emma. "I know how hard you've tried with Sammy, but he might not be the right cat for us after all. He needs to go to a rescue, I think. Where they have people who are used to taking care of cats like him."

"I'm not sure," Dad said. "I know Sammy was difficult when we brought him home, but he is getting better."

"Getting better!" Mom stared at him. "Emma is covered in scratches!"

"I don't think it's that big of a deal," Aunt Grace said gently. "Even Whiskers scratches me sometimes if I go to pick him up and he just doesn't feel like it."

Mom sighed again. "I'm sorry, Emma, but he's too unpredictable. I'm not sure he's ever going to be really friendly. Maybe he needs a home more like the stables, where he doesn't have to be around people if he doesn't want to."

"Mom, please don't send him away!" Emma wailed. "I don't want any other cat, only Sammy! He'll be fine, I know he will. I'll do anything to keep him." She stared pleadingly at her mom, tears trickling down her cheeks. She couldn't bear the thought of poor Sammy going to a rescue—somewhere else strange and new and frightening. He'd have to start all over again, and soon it would be too late to tame him. He'd be shy and wild forever.

"Just give us a few more weeks, honey," Dad suggested. "Of course today's a little bit of a setback, but we have to keep trying."

"Two more weeks." Mom looked from Emma to Dad and back again. "We should be able to tell by then, shouldn't we?"

Dad nodded slowly. "All right. Emma?"

"I guess so," Emma whispered huskily. She was so upset that her voice seemed to have disappeared. Two weeks! It was no time at all.

"What's the matter?" Keira asked as she led Jasmine past Emma and Sparky. "Is Sparky being a pain about getting tacked up again? You look, well, a little sad...," she trailed off, not sure what to say. Emma looked like she might be about to cry.

"No." Emma sniffed. "Actually Sparky's been great. Maybe he can tell I just can't deal with a mischievous pony today."

"Oh, no! What is it?" Keira swapped Jasmine's reins to her other hand and gave Emma a hug. "Don't cry!"

"I can't help it." Emma's voice shook. "Mom says we might have to give Sammy to a rescue. She thinks we can't handle him."

"But wasn't it going really well?" Keira said, confused. "You showed me that photo your dad took of him eating off your fingers. He looked so happy."

"He's still jumpy, though," Emma gulped. "Mom thinks he's not going to adapt to living in a house. He got scared last night because my aunt was there, and he scratched me. I didn't mind—not much—but Mom was really upset about it. She says we have two weeks to prove he can be a pet, or he has to go." She was crying so much that she could hardly get the last words out.

Keira hugged her tighter, and even Sparky and Jasmine leaned in close, as if they wanted to make Emma feel better.

"Two weeks is a long time," Keira said. "Honestly, it really is. And I saw how friendly and tame he was with you here. You almost had me petting him, Emma, and I'm scared of cats!"

"I guess so…," Emma said, between gasps. "It doesn't feel like long, though. If he goes to a rescue, he'll be all lost and alone. It'll be awful."

"Then you absolutely have to make sure it doesn't happen," Keira said firmly. "I'll see if I can think of anything to help." She gave Emma one last hug. "Ems, we have to go. Liz is waving at us. She wants us to try those dressage aids today, remember?"

Emma nodded and sniffed hard. "I'm okay. I'm so glad I told you about it, Keira. I do actually feel a little happier."

Emma grabbed her riding hat from the back seat and looked anxiously at Aunt Grace's purple car parked outside their house.

"It's all right," Dad said soothingly. "She said she wouldn't go near Sammy. Although we will have to try and get him used to meeting new people eventually. She has something for you."

Emma hurried down the path, curious to see what Aunt Grace had brought. She had a feeling it was something important—not just a magazine or some chocolate to cheer her up, but something that really mattered.

"Emma! I'm so glad you got back before I had to go to work. Look, I brought you this." Aunt Grace whirled out of the front door onto the path. "Here. I really hope it helps."

Emma looked down at the book that her aunt had pressed into her hands—*Taming Feral Kittens*. There was a sweet little orange kitten on the front of it, with a shy, worried look on its face that made Emma think of Sammy at once.

"I got it at the rescue center. I thought I'd go and ask them if they had any tips for you. They were so friendly and helpful. This was written by someone who used to work there, and they said to call if you get really stuck. I wrote the number inside the cover for you." She hugged Emma. "Sweetheart, if Sammy does have to go there, they will take good care of him, I promise."

Emma nodded. "But it's not going to happen," she said firmly. "This is terrific, Aunt Grace. Thank you! I'm going to go and read it now."

Sammy sat in the doorway of the crate, looking out suspiciously. Everything was different—the crate had been moved down onto the floor, and he didn't like that, for starters. He preferred to be high up, so he could see who was coming. High up was safe.

But he liked the open door. He thought he did, anyway. He sniffed the air beyond the crate, his whiskers twitching. He could step out, right onto the floor. He could explore. Cautiously, he extended one paw over the door frame, and then the next, and then his two back paws.

He stood nervously just outside the crate, watching, scanning the room. Emma was there, sitting in the corner, and her dad was over by the counter. She wasn't looking at him—she was gazing off into the distance as if she hadn't noticed what he was doing. Sammy took a few steps out into the room and sniffed.

Food! He could definitely smell food. He was sure it was well past his usual feeding time. He'd been expecting Emma to bring food, but instead she and her dad had put his crate down onto the floor. Determinedly, he stomped across the floor toward the smell. Emma had his bowl on her lap. He stopped a few steps away from her, looking uncertainly at the bowl. He wasn't sure he wanted to go any closer, but he was hungry.

His tail swished from side to side, and then he made a panicked little run, flinging himself at the bowl. What if she took it away? Sammy climbed up on Emma's leg and started to gobble down the food as quickly as he could.

"It's all right," Emma whispered. "I'm not going anywhere."

Sammy's ears flickered, but he didn't stop eating. Then he felt her petting him, very gently running her hand over his shoulders and down his back. It was nice—it felt like his mother licking him. He slowed his eating down a little, almost sure that the bowl wasn't going to be taken away.

At last, he'd finished the entire bowl. He licked around it carefully and then sniffed it to make sure there wasn't any more. There wasn't, but he was full anyway.

Slowly, carefully, he settled down into a crouch on Emma's lap. She was still petting him, so gently. Sammy stretched out his paws and kneaded them up and down on Emma's skirt. Then he closed his eyes and purred.

Chapter Eight
Home Sweet Home

Emma tucked the phone under her chin so she could talk to Aunt Grace and have both hands free for scrambling after the ping-pong ball as Sammy sent it skittering around all over the floor.

"It really works," she told her aunt, a little breathlessly. "We started on Sunday after I'd had time to read the book. All this week, we've only fed him with the bowl on me or Dad, so that he has to come to us to get his food. And he's always hungry, so it works perfectly. The very first time we tried it, he let me pet him, and he even purred! I'm starting to think he actually does like me," she added shyly.

"Of course he does. Oh, that's wonderful, Emma! I felt awful when your mom said you might have to give him up."

"Me, too. But I'm hoping she's going to let me keep him. She was laughing at him this morning when he was playing with his feathery toy before school. He was trying to catch it so hard that he kept almost falling over backward." Emma threw the ping-pong ball again for Sammy. "We're doing the next thing it says in the book now. He's going to be allowed out in the kitchen all the time, not just for food time and playing. His bed and his litter box are still in the crate, but we'll leave it open so he can come and go when he wants to."

"And then I suppose you'll bring his bed out, and eventually get rid of the crate?"

"Exactly. I don't know how long it's going to take, though. The book says it depends on the kitten. Oh, Sammy!"

"What did he do?" Aunt Grace laughed at the other end of the line.

"He chased after the ball so fast that he ran into the cupboard. He's fine; he just looks a little confused. Hold on just a minute." Emma laid the phone on the floor and wriggled closer to Sammy, whispering comforting noises. She was sure that he looked embarrassed, if a kitten could. His ears had gone flat.

"It's okay," she whispered and without thinking about it, she scooped Sammy gently into her hands and snuggled him up against her sweater. "Oh... I didn't mean to...." It was the first time she'd ever picked him up. But Sammy hadn't clawed her, or jumped away in fright. He was huddled against her, so tiny and fragile that she could feel his heart beating under her fingers. "You don't mind?" she said. "Oh, Sammy, I do love you...."

"Hey...," Dad whispered from the doorway. "He looks happy!"

"Dad, can you pick up the phone?" Emma whispered. "I was talking to

Aunt Grace. She must be wondering what happened to me. Can you please tell her I'll call her later?"

Dad chuckled. "Sure. I'll tell her you're occupied with some very important business."

"Are you sure?" Emma looked worriedly at Keira. "I mean, I'd love it if you came over for lunch. But I know how you feel about cats."

"Exactly," Keira called back as she hefted Jasmine's saddle over to the tackroom. "And so does your mom. So if even silly Keira isn't scared of playing with Sammy, he must be okay as a pet, right? The two weeks are up, aren't they? We need to show your mom how good Sammy is."

"Two weeks yesterday. I haven't wanted to ask Mom what's happening." Emma sighed. "And I never said you were silly," she added quickly.

Keira grinned. "I know. But I am silly.

I can't even say what it is that makes me frightened of cats. They just make me so nervous."

"I don't want you to be miserable." Emma frowned. "And…." She nibbled her bottom lip. "If you're nervous, it might make Sammy nervous, too," she explained. "He was all right with Aunt Grace when she came over during the week. She was really good. She just sat on the floor completely still until he was brave enough to sniff at her. But she's used to cats, and she wasn't scared."

"I won't be scared, either," Keira said. "I promise. I said I'd try to think of something I could do to help, and this is it. I'll be brave." She smiled at Emma. "Honestly. I'll be fine."

"He's in here, in the kitchen." Emma looked back at Keira. She could see her mom hovering behind her friend with an anxious expression on her face. Mom obviously wasn't sure about this—neither was Emma, to be honest. But Keira seemed so certain. She'd explained to Emma's mom in the car that she wanted to try and stop being scared of cats, and that she knew she'd be okay with Sammy because he was so little.

Emma opened the door slowly and peered around. "Oh, he's asleep in his basket. Actually, that's good. How about we sit on the floor for a while? We can have a snack, and then when he wakes up, we can let him come and see you."

Keira nodded. Emma thought she looked pale. But she looked determined, too. "That's a good idea."

Emma took her hand, pulling her gently into the kitchen to sit down half under the table. That would give Sammy plenty of space to get a good look at them before he got out of his basket. Keira even giggled when Emma's mom handed them a plate of cheese cubes and apple to eat under there. "It's like being really small and making tents under the table. Did you ever do that?" she whispered.

"Yes! Hey, I think he's waking up." Emma glanced at her. "Sure you're all right?"

"Mm-hmm."

Emma could feel Keira tensing up beside her. Maybe it was a bad idea, after all. But it was too late to do anything about it now.

Sammy stretched and yawned, and popped his head up out of his basket to see what was happening. He was hungry, and he could smell something delicious. Not his regular food, but that only made it more exciting. He twitched his ears forward and gazed at Emma under the table. Emma and someone else. He flicked his tail from side to side worriedly. It wasn't someone he knew, but she was sitting very still. She had some of whatever it was that smelled so nice; he could see it in her hands. And she was holding it very close to the floor....

Sammy hopped out of his basket and set off across the floor, his whiskers trembling as he smelled the cheese. He nudged his head against Emma's feet on the way, as if to say that she belonged to him. But he was still more interested in the cheese. He padded between Emma's legs and the new girl's, and sniffed hopefully at the girl's fingers. She was holding that piece of cheese as if she didn't really want it at all.

He froze for a second, ears flickering, expecting someone to shoo him away. But no one did. Swiftly, Sammy grabbed the scrap out of her hand and gulped it down, savoring every crumb.

Then he licked Keira's fingers, just to check that he hadn't missed any. He felt her laugh—her fingers shook—but there was no more cheese. He gave her one last lick and turned to scramble up into Emma's lap. He could still smell cheese, and he was sure that if Emma had any, she'd give it to him. He hauled himself up her leggings, breathing hard, and half fell into her lap. Then he sat there and gave a huge yawn, showing all his tiny sharp teeth and his raspberry-pink tongue.

"He's beautiful," Keira whispered, sounding surprised.

"You didn't mind when he licked you?" Emma asked. She couldn't stop smiling—Sammy had perched himself on her lap like he belonged.

Keira wrinkled her nose. "Actually, I was really scared. But he's so little— I just kept thinking I could run out if I couldn't deal with it."

"Oh, Keira," Emma's mom whispered. "Do you want to go into the other room?"

Keira shook her head. "No, I think it's okay," she said cautiously. "He's really good."

Emma's mom nodded. "I guess he is." She smiled at Emma. "So, are you having lunch under the table, then?"

"I don't think we'd actually get much of our lunch if we did that." Slowly, carefully, Emma moved onto her knees, cuddling Sammy against her fleece top as she stood up and went to sit on one of the kitchen chairs. She was waiting for him to leap away, but Sammy only stretched his neck out so he could peer over the edge of the table at the plate of sandwiches that her mom was putting down.

Keira laughed. "He's eyeing the food as though you never feed him, Emma."

"He can't think he's making a habit of sitting on your lap at mealtimes," Mom said sternly. "Just this once."

Emma stared at her delightedly. "You mean...."

Her mom nodded. "Yes—I was

talking to your dad about it last night. Sammy's so much happier now. Oh, Emma, watch out! He's going for that ham sandwich!" She quickly pulled the plate back, and Sammy looked disappointed.

"I'll get you some in a minute," Emma whispered in his ear. "A whole sandwich, if you like!"

Sammy yawned again and purred a little and rubbed his face against her hand. Then he nuzzled at Emma's top, and pawed his way gently over the zipper, snuggling down inside.

Emma looked down lovingly at the little tabby kitten curled up inside her fleece. "Sammy, you're staying!"

The Brave Kitten

Contents

For Helena and her beautiful cat Karmel, whose story I borrowed for this book

Chapter One
The Discovery

"We'd better hurry, Helena," Lucy said, glancing at her watch and walking faster. "There's a lot to do this morning, with two dogs coming in to be operated on. I need to get everything ready."

"I'll help," Helena said cheerfully, twirling along the pavement in front of her cousin. Helping out at the animal hospital was her favorite. "I can do the feeding and clean the cages on my own. I know what I'm doing."

Lucy grinned at her. "I know you do. You're like the youngest veterinary nurse in the country, Helena—you've had almost as much practice as me."

"I haven't decided yet what I want to be—whether I should be a nurse, or an actual vet," Helena said seriously. "Being a vet's harder. And I'm not sure about doing operations. I don't really like blood. But maybe I'd get used to it."

"You do," Lucy said. "I didn't like it much when I first started training as a nurse, but now it doesn't bother me at all."

"I suppose that cute, lop-eared rabbit has already gone home?" Helena asked. She'd loved petting the rabbit when she'd gone to see Lucy at the animal hospital after school a couple of days earlier. "He was so friendly and— Lucy, what's that?" Helena stopped dancing along the pavement and peered worriedly at the parked car up ahead of them. There was a little mound of pale, sandy fur tucked just underneath the car.

"Oh, no…," Lucy muttered. "Helena, don't look, okay? Just wait there."

"What is it?" Helena asked. She was suddenly feeling a little bit sick, and her heart was jumping. She didn't want to go closer and see whatever it was. But at the same time, she couldn't just stay back. The little heap of fur looked like a cat to her, but cats didn't usually lie sprawled like that, not on a road, anyway. Only if they were somewhere warm and safe. "Is it a cat?" she whispered miserably to Lucy, coming closer. "Has it been run over?"

Lucy glanced back at her, frowning, but she could see that Helena wasn't going to stay out of the way. Her cousin loved cats, even though she didn't have one of her own. "I think so. Don't cry, Helena. It must have been quick."

But Helena wasn't listening. "Lucy, look! He moved! I'm sure he did."

Lucy whipped around. The little cat had been so cold and lifeless that she hadn't thought he could still be alive, but Helena was right. He'd twitched, just a bit. "Oh, wow...," she muttered. "We need to get him to the hospital, now. Molly and Pete should be in soon—he's definitely going to need a vet to look at him."

"How are we going to get him there, though? Won't it hurt him if we pick him up?" Helena crouched down by the car, peering at the little cat. One of his back legs was really swollen and seemed to be at a funny angle, and she could hardly see him breathing at all. But his eyes were open now, just a tiny slit of

273

gold. He was looking at them.

"Yes," Lucy admitted. "And he might not want us to touch him, either. But we need to get him there quickly. He's in shock, and I've got a feeling he's been here for a while—he's so cold." She pulled off her big scarf and gently wrapped it around the cat, scooping him up and trying to support the injured leg as well as she could.

Helena watched, biting her lip. She'd seen cats at the hospital hissing and scratching at Lucy and the vets because they were frightened or hurting. She hoped this cat wasn't going to fight— he didn't look as though he had the strength.

Maybe he was just too weak, or maybe he understood that Lucy and Helena were trying to help, but the cat lay still in Lucy's arms as they hurried down the street. Helena was jogging beside Lucy, carrying her bag and looking up at the cat. His head was drooping over Lucy's arm, and from time to time his mouth opened in a tiny, soundless meow.

"You might be hurting him," Helena told Lucy worriedly.

"I know. But we're almost there. Look, I can see Molly's car. She's here already."

Helena pushed open the animal hospital door and looked around. Molly must be out back somewhere, or upstairs making coffee.

"Helena, you hold him." Lucy carefully passed over the scarf-wrapped bundle. "Take him into the back room. I'll go and find Molly."

Helena stood there helplessly. The cat hardly weighed anything at all, and he wasn't moving. She had an awful feeling he wasn't going to survive—he was too weak. "Just hold on," she whispered as she carried him to the room where Molly and Pete operated. She wondered if she should put him down on the table, but she didn't want to. The table was cold and hard, and she wanted the cat to know that somebody loved him. "Just hold on, *please*.... We're going to make you better."

The golden cat opened his eyes and gazed up at her. He didn't understand what was going on. Everything seemed to hurt, and he was frightened. He still wasn't sure what had happened—there had been bright lights suddenly flashing out of the darkness and so much noise. He didn't remember anything after that, until he had woken up at the side of the road and his legs wouldn't work properly.

He had wanted so much to go home, to curl up in his basket, and hide until he felt better. But he was so dizzy and sick, he wasn't really sure where home was. And it hurt to move. He couldn't walk; one of his back legs wasn't working at all, and the other one ached. He could only do a strange sort of hop, dragging his bad leg behind him. He'd managed to get a little way up the road, but then he'd felt so cold and tired, he'd hidden under the parked car. Once he'd lain down, it just seemed too hard to get up again.

Now he could feel the warmth of the girl's arms around him. He liked the softness of her voice, too. She sounded gentle, and he rubbed his head against her arm, just a little, to show her he was grateful. But it hurt too much to do anything more, and his eyes flickered closed again.

"Lucy, he woke up a bit, but now I think he's getting worse!" Helena said anxiously as Lucy and Molly clattered down the stairs and into the operating room. "He's gone really limp. Please say you can help him, Molly. He's such a sweet cat. He hasn't hissed or scratched or anything."

Molly took the cat and laid him carefully on the table. "Definitely a broken leg," she said. "But it's the shock that's really dangerous at the moment. Let's get him on a drip. That'll get some fluids back into him," she explained, seeing Helena frown. "It's a little bit like you having one of those energy drinks after you've been running."

"Oh." Helena nodded, wishing the cat would open his eyes again. He looked so weak. He hadn't even flinched when Molly had moved him.

"Once he's warmed up, we can examine him," Molly explained. "I don't want to bother him with X-rays while he's like this. But we can at least check if he's got a microchip, and if he does, we can call his owner."

Lucy passed her the microchip scanner and Molly held it above the cat's neck—but it didn't beep. It didn't make any sound at all.

"No chip," Molly sighed. "Oh, well. We can put a sign up in the hospital window, I suppose."

"But what if his owners never find out where he is?" Helena asked, her voice shaking a little. Life seemed so hard for the poor cat—run over, and now maybe homeless as well.

"Once they realize he's missing, I'm sure they'll call the local vets," Lucy told her comfortingly. But she glanced at Molly. "Are we going to be okay to operate?" she asked. "I mean, he is very skinny. If he's a stray...."

Molly nodded, frowning. "I know. We could send him over to the rescue center—they'd treat him. But he's so wobbly already, I don't think it's a good idea to move him."

"Why can't you fix his leg here?" Helena asked. She didn't understand what was going on. Surely they needed to operate on the cat as soon as they could! Helena knew that Molly sometimes worked as a volunteer vet at the recue center, which helped pets whose owners had problems paying for expensive vet treatments. But why did the cat have to go there?

Lucy put an arm around Helena's shoulders. "It depends on the X-ray,  but he might need to have the broken leg pinned," she explained. "It's a really expensive operation, and then he's going to need to be taken care of for a while. Plus he'll have to have another operation to take the pins out. If he's a stray, there's no one to pay for all that, or for his medicine."

"And even if he does have an owner, they might not be able to afford the treatment." Molly ran her hand over the cat's caramel-colored ears, looking sad.

"You mean, you might not be able to

do the operation?" Helena whispered. "Even if it would make him better?"

"Of course we want to help him," Molly explained. "He's young enough to recover really well. But...."

"You have to!" Helena's eyes filled with tears as she rubbed the cat under the chin. "He's so sweet. He nuzzled me.... He's trusting us to take care of him!"

"I bet the rescue center would help take care of him while he's getting better," Molly said, eyeing the cat thoughtfully. "They might cover the costs if we have to operate, too." She crouched down to be eye to eye with the caramel cat, and gave a firm little nod. "We have to help him."

Chapter Two
Recovering

The caramel-colored cat lay in his cage, staring out at the dimly lit room. He didn't understand where he was, or what was happening. He was dazed, and he felt sick. And there was still something wrong with his leg. It felt worse, if anything. It was aching and heavy, and he couldn't move it properly. It smelled wrong, too—strange and sharp with chemicals. He hated it. Wearily, he pulled himself up on his front legs so he could look at his back leg. It was that weird white wrapping all over his leg that smelled odd.

He leaned over, wincing as the weight pressed on the broken leg, and pulled with his teeth at the bandage that lined the cast. If he could just get that off, then his leg would be all right again, he was certain....

"I wasn't sure you'd be up yet!" said Lucy, smiling at Helena, who was standing outside her front door with her coat on, looking impatient.

"Mom still has her pajamas on,"

Helena admitted, pointing over her shoulder, and Lucy spotted her aunt waving at her out of the kitchen window. "I know it's early, but I really want to see how the cat is."

"I'm sure he'll be fine," Lucy said. "Molly stayed overnight, remember. One of the vets always does when there's a serious case, and she was worried about him. There's a bed upstairs, and she'll have popped down every couple of hours to check on him. 'Bye, Aunt Claire!" she called to Helena's mom. "I'll drop her off in time for lunch—I'm only going in to help Molly out this morning. I hope she's managed to get some sleep," Lucy added to Helena. "That bed's really lumpy. We'll go and make her a cup of coffee and some toast."

But when they got to the animal hospital, Molly was already up, and she looked upset when she opened the front door for them.

"What's wrong?" Lucy asked.

"I don't know how he did it." Molly shook her head in frustration. "I checked on him a couple of hours ago, and he was still dozing. He looked fine. But I've just been in, and he's pulled the cast off." She sighed. "We went with a cast because it was a fairly simple break, but at this rate, he's going to make it worse."

"Can you put another cast on?" Helena asked as they followed Molly inside.

"We'll have to. But the more he messes around with that leg, the longer it's going to take to heal. We'll just have to keep an eye on him. He'll probably need a cone collar on now to keep him from trying to tug the cast off, but he'll hate it, and he's pretty miserable already. This time I'm going to use a special kind of cast that tastes horrible if cats try to chew it, so I'm hoping he'll just leave it alone."

"Poor little cat," Helena said, looking into the small cage where the kitten was stretched out on a blanket. He looked back at her wearily, and she could see how sad he was. He was squashed right into the corner of the cage, as if he was trying to hide from everyone. "I bet he hates being shut up in here."

"He needs to be kept still, though," Lucy explained. "Even if he went home, he'd have to stay in a small room—maybe even a dog crate or something—to keep him from doing something silly."

"Has anyone called about him?" Helena asked Molly hopefully. "His owners?"

Molly shook her head. "No, no one's called. I'd better put up a flyer."

"I could make some on the computer," Helena suggested. "We could print them out and put them up close to where we found him, too. His owners must be really worried about him." She shivered, thinking about how wonderful it would be to have a cat of her very own, and how frightened she'd feel if he simply disappeared.

"Posters would be good." Molly nodded. "Okay. Plaster cast number two...."

"Please don't try and pull this one off," Helena whispered to the cat. He was back in his cage with the new cast on, and she'd brought him some food and water. "And don't put your foot in the water bowl, either. When I broke my arm, I wasn't allowed to get it wet at all."

She crouched down on the floor in front of the cage. There were six of them, in two rows on top of each other, and the caramel cat was in one of the bottom ones. "You look really miserable," Helena told him. "Aren't you going to have any breakfast?" She was whispering, and trying not to stare the cat in the eyes. She knew he wouldn't like it.

Even though Helena didn't have a cat, Grandma had given her a book all about cats last Christmas. It was because Helena had told Grandma her secret Christmas wish, when Grandma had asked what present she might like. What Helena really wanted for Christmas was a cat, but it was a secret because Helena knew that Mom would never let her have one. She'd asked before, a lot of times, and Mom had always said no. Helena could sort of see why—her mom was a teacher at the school Helena went to, so they were both out all day. A kitten would be lonely and bored and miserable, and Mom thought it wasn't fair. Helena couldn't help thinking that she could make the rest of the time so special that the kitten wouldn't mind. But she knew Mom wouldn't agree.

Grandma had given Helena a tiny china cat and the book, which had a lot of beautiful photos and all kinds of things one needed to know to be a cat owner. She'd written in the front that Helena might not need it right now, but she would have a cat of her own one day. And meanwhile, please could she come and practice with Grandma's cats, Snow and Smudge, as they were getting big and needed Helena to play with them!

On Saturday, Helena had gone home and read everything she could find about cat injuries. After she'd read everything there was in the book from Grandma, she'd gone online to look up more information. Now she was worried that the cat was traumatized by the accident. She'd had to get her mom to explain what traumatized meant. It was that the memory of the accident and the time at the vet's might make the cat really upset, and maybe not very friendly.

That made a lot of sense to Helena. She'd broken her arm falling off the jungle gym at school, and even though that had been a year ago, she'd never gone back on the jungle gym.

Hopefully, if she made the little caramel cat's stay at the vet's as nice as possible, he'd think about that, rather than the car, and the cage, and his leg hurting. *It had to be worth a try*, Helena thought.

The cat sniffed at the food, and even though cats didn't really shrug or sigh, Helena was almost sure he did. *I just can't be bothered*, he was thinking—she could tell. He didn't even eat a mouthful.

Slowly, Helena reached into the cage and tickled him under the chin with one finger. He was such a handsome cat, even with the ugly plaster on his leg—a soft peachy color all over, with darker caramel stripes, and no white on him at all, except for his drooping whiskers. His nose was apricot-pink, and his eyes were huge and golden. *He is going to be big*, Helena thought, *when he is fully grown*. His paws were enormous, as though he needed to grow into them.

The cat curled himself into her hand a little, enjoying the soft touch of the girl's fingers. He didn't understand why he was here, shut up in this cage. The white thing was back on his leg again and now it smelled even worse, if that was possible. And it had tasted disgusting when he'd tried chewing at it. This whole place smelled wrong. Too clean. He hated it. He wanted to go back to his house and his yard, and his little patch of street. But he didn't know where home was—he hadn't known for a while. He'd gone exploring and then, somehow, he hadn't known how to get back home. He didn't understand it—he had thought he would always know. But it had been a long time now, and he'd been hungry and tired and frightened when he tried to cross that road. Now he was farther away from his home than ever.

He almost felt like whipping his head around and nipping at the girl's fingers with his teeth. But not quite. That patch under his chin was his favorite place to be petted, and she wasn't stopping. She'd reached all the itchy parts now, and he wheezed out the faintest breath of a purr.

"Oh! Are you purring?" Helena whispered. "Are you feeling better?" She ran her hand gently over his smooth head and sighed. "If you don't have an owner, you'll have to go to the rescue center when you're better so they can take care of you until someone wants you. I hope you cheer up before then, caramel cat. You're so beautiful, and I think you'd be a wonderful pet. But no one's going to take you home if you just hide at the back of your cage. You'll end up staying at the rescue for a long time."

The little golden cat stayed flopped on his blanket, and Helena tried not to think, *Maybe forever*....

Chapter Three
Worrying

"So how's the cat now?" Helena's friend Katie asked. "I suppose you haven't seen him since yesterday."

"No, and I bet Mom's going to say it's too late to stop by the animal hospital on the way home," Helena sighed. They were waiting for Helena's mom to come over from the staff room to pick them up from soccer after school.

She usually dropped Katie off at home, too, or sometimes Katie stayed for a snack. "She did let me text Lucy last night, and Lucy said he hadn't taken the cast off again. He still hadn't tried standing up, though, and he hadn't eaten much."

"And nobody knows who he belongs to?" Katie asked anxiously. "Poor little cat! What's going to happen to him?"

Helena sighed. "Lucy said that if no one claims him in another day or so, he'll have to go to the rescue. But I don't think anyone's going to want a limpy, miserable cat who won't even come and say hello, even if he is pretty. They're putting a photo of him in the local paper, too. Maybe his owner will see that."

"Sorry I'm late! Are you telling Katie about the cat?" Helena's mom had hurried up behind the girls without them noticing. "I wonder if they've found his owner yet."

"That's just what we were talking about," Helena said with a tiny sigh. Of course, she did want the cat to go back to his old home. But a little bit of her was imagining him coming home with her instead.

"Don't worry, Helena," her mom said gently. "Even if he has to go to the rescue, it'll be fine. I know quite a few people who've gotten their cats and dogs from there. The animals are taken care of really well, and the staff works hard to find new homes for them."

"I suppose so," Helena sighed.

Katie gave her a sympathetic look—she realized what Helena was wishing. Her family had a big black Labrador named Charlie, and Helena loved to come with her to walk him. Katie knew how much her friend wanted a pet of her own.

Lucy called Helena that evening while she was helping her mom make dinner.

"Has anyone called the hospital

about the cat?" Helena asked her cousin hopefully. "Is he okay?"

"He's eating a little better, but no, still no sign of an owner." There was a little silence, and then Lucy added, "I told Molly I'd take him home with me in a couple of days. Then I can try to find a home for him when he's better. I haven't broken it to Mom and Dad yet, though."

"Oh, that's great!" Helena squealed, so loudly that her mom almost dropped a pan of pasta. Lucy lived with her mom and dad and her younger twin sisters, and their house wasn't far from Helena's. She'd still be able to see the cat all the time. She could go and visit him.

"I wasn't sure the staff at the rescue

would have time to take care of him properly. He needs a lot of TLC, poor thing."

"Definitely," Helena agreed. "Can I stop over with Grandma after my dance class tomorrow? It'll be just as you're cleaning everything up to go home. You know how much Grandma loves cats. I told her about him."

Lucy giggled. "I'm surprised she hasn't been around already. See you tomorrow then!"

"Here he is—he's a little quiet still." Helena pointed to the caramel-colored cat, huddled in the back of the cage and staring out at Helena's grandma rather grumpily. But he shuffled toward the front of the cage when he saw Helena, and she giggled. "That's right. You'd better be nice—I've brought you a present. Look." She pulled a packet of cat treats out of her pocket and ripped the foil. "Tuna flavor! I think they smell awful, but the websites I looked at said most cats love the fishy ones."

"Beautiful colors in his fur...," Grandma said. "So when are you taking him home, Lucy?"

"Tomorrow, I think." Lucy crouched down to look at the cat with them. "He really needs to get out of that little cage and start exercising his leg some more now that it's beginning to heal. He's going to live in the laundry room."

"What did your mom and dad say about it?" Helena asked.

Lucy made a face. "They weren't very happy.... But I explained about the rescue being so busy, and I promised we weren't keeping him forever. Mom says I have to do all the laundry if there's going to be a cat living in the laundry room...."

"Are you finishing work now, Lucy?"

Grandma said, looking at her watch. "Do you want a ride home? I haven't seen Emily and Bella for at least a week. We could stop in and say hello."

Emily and Bella were Lucy's little sisters, and Helena's cousins. They were only four. Helena loved going to see them—they were always so funny. Usually when she went over there, she was talked into having her hair done in some crazy style, covered in feathers or glitter.

But sitting in the back of the car, she couldn't help thinking about the cat—so quiet and sad. How was he going to get along with two crazy four year olds? Not to mention Lucy's dog, Buster. He was about as silly as Emily and Bella, and he chased cats, too.

Helena had seen Lucy hanging on to the end of his leash for dear life when they were out for a walk and a cat strolled by.

Helena hugged Emily and Bella when they jumped on her in the hallway, and let them drag her upstairs and paint her nails bright blue. (Mom would make her take it off again before school, but that was okay.) But she didn't enjoy her visit to her cousins' house as much as she usually did.

She just couldn't imagine that frightened little cat living here, even for a little while. Buster was a terrific dog (Emily and Bella had painted his nails blue, too, and he'd let them), but Helena was sure that if he could smell a cat on the other side of the laundry room door, he wouldn't rest until he'd clawed that door to shreds. It wasn't fair to Buster, either. And the caramel cat would be much too nervous to let Emily and Bella draw pictures all over his cast with sparkly pens.

It wasn't going to work.

"What's wrong, Helena?" Grandma asked as they got back into the car. "You're so quiet."

"The cat…," Helena said worriedly. "I'm not sure he'll be able to cope with

Lucy's house, Grandma. I'm not being mean—it's just that he's still so nervous, and there's so much going on there. I think it'll make him worse."

Grandma sighed. "I was thinking about that, too. But Lucy said he'll be kept in one room...."

"Yeah, but there's no way Emily and Bella will leave him in there," Helena pointed out. "They'll be dressing him in their dolls' clothes the minute Aunt Sam's back is turned."

"Mmmm." Grandma drove down the road, frowning to herself. "I wish I could take him...."

"Snow and Smudge wouldn't like it, though, would they?" Helena sighed. "Everyone already has cats, or dogs, or twins." She was silent for a minute, and then added, "Except us. Me and Mom. Mom's always said no, because it wouldn't be good for a cat to be left alone, but this cat needs to have some peace and quiet. Don't you think so, Grandma?"

"And I could always stop in and see him at lunchtime. Give him some attention." Grandma darted a hopeful glance at Helena. "You know, maybe we could persuade your mom together."

"She already said he was beautiful when Lucy showed her the photo on her phone." Helena wound her hands together, over and over. She was suddenly so excited she couldn't keep still.

They just had to convince her mom….

Chapter Four
The Perfect Plan

"But we can't.... We don't have anywhere to keep him."

"We do, Mom! In here—in the kitchen would be all right. He couldn't jump on the counter. We could put a blanket in that space under the counter for him, with his food bowls and litter box, and I promise I'll clean it out."

"I can come and check on him at lunchtime, Claire," Grandma suggested.

Helena's mom frowned, looking around at her little kitchen.

"He can't go to Lucy's house, Mom," said Helena. "And he'll be miserable at the rescue, I know he will. No one's come to claim him, even though we put posters up all around where we found him, and in the animal hospital window. He's in the paper today, with a message saying to call the hospital, but no one has yet. Maybe his owner will see the photo, but he was so thin, Lucy thinks that could mean he's been a stray for a while. I want to be able to take care of him. It feels like I have to, since I was the one who found him."

Helena's mom was silent for a moment, then she turned around to look at her daughter. "I suppose so. Oh, Helena. It's going to be a lot of work, you know. But I am proud of you."

"You mean … yes?" Helena asked, confused. She'd expected to have to beg for an awful lot longer than that. And even then, deep down, she'd been almost certain that her mom would never agree.

"Yes. I mean, we'll have to give him back if his owner contacts the hospital, but yes. Do you think he could stay there until the weekend?" her mom asked. "Then we'd have two whole days to get him used to being at our house before we have to leave him on his own."

The cat was sitting up the next afternoon when Helena brought her mom to meet him. He peered out of the cage bars, waiting for her. He could hear her talking to someone in the next room, and she sounded excited and happy. She had brought him cat treats the last time she came, fishy ones that he liked.

And sometimes she opened the front of the cage and sat for a while, rubbing his fur and talking to him. She made him feel safe. Even when he was stuck here in this place that wasn't his home, and he could smell the dogs at the other end of the room.

He sat up, wondering if maybe she'd let him out of the cage this time. He could sit on her, and then she'd be able to pet him better and rub his ears.

When he saw the girl come in, he skittered nervously back, knocking his cast against the floor of the cage. She wasn't alone—

the young woman was with her, the one he saw every day, and someone else, too.

"It's all right," Helena said soothingly. "This is my mom. We'll be taking you home to our house soon...."

The caramel cat didn't know what Helena was saying, but he liked hearing her soft voice. And the other person spoke softly, too.

"He's beautiful, Helena. Even more so than in the pictures. What are we going to call him? Or have you named him already?"

Helena opened the door of the cage, and the cat stepped out slowly, sniffing at her outstretched hand. She rubbed the dark caramel stripes between his ears and smiled at her mom.

"I haven't really named him. But when I think about him, I call him the cat with the caramel fur. Do you think we could call him Caramel?"

"We're here!" Helena said gratefully, turning around to peer at the cat carrier strapped into the back seat. Caramel had been howling dismally ever since Mom drove off. He clearly hated the carrier, and didn't like the feeling of the moving car at all.

"Do you think being in a car reminds him of the accident?" she asked her mom worriedly.

"No. I think all cats hate being in boxes. Shut in them, I mean. They like getting in by themselves." Her mom turned off the engine and looked around, too. "Even when he's been in the cage at the vet's for an entire week, it's not the same. He can't see out of that carrier very well. He'll be much better when we let him into the kitchen."

"It'll probably feel huge," Helena agreed, opening her door and going to get the cat carrier out of the back. "We're here, Caramel. This is your house now, too. Just your kitchen for the minute, though. But Molly says you'll be able to have the cast off in about three more weeks, since you're still a kitten, and you'll heal quicker than a big cat." She carried the box into the house as she talked to him, and her mom came in behind her, shutting the door of their little kitchen. There were only the countertops in there, and the oven and the fridge, and Helena was almost sure Caramel wouldn't be able to jump up on those. So it was a safe place to keep him.

"Look," she said gently, unlatching the top of the box and taking it off so Caramel could decide to come out when he wanted to. "There's a special soft basket for you. And a litter box. And I'll get you some food."

They had gone to the pet store the

night before and got it all—the travel carrier, and the basket with a cushion, and the food and water bowls. It had been so exciting. Helena had looked at cat toys as well, but they hadn't bought any, not right now. They were all designed for chasing and rolling and batting with paws, and Caramel needed to stay quiet and rest. Helena promised herself she'd go back and get him some of those toys once he was better.

Caramel sat pressed against the back of the carrier, looking around suspiciously. He hadn't understood what was happening when they'd lifted him out of the cage and into this horrible little crate. Then he'd thought that maybe they were going home. It had been such a long time since he'd been there.

He hunched his shoulders, ears laid back, and watched Helena and her mom both watching him. But they were quiet and still, and no one was grabbing at him. The fur along his spine flattened down a little, and he padded his paws thoughtfully into the blanket. Then he sniffed and shook his ears, standing up a bit lopsided. This wasn't his old house, of course. But it smelled good. Not like the pet hospital, full of sharp, strong smells that hurt his nose. This place smelled like the girl, and food. He lurched out of the basket, his plastered leg tangling in the blanket, and set out to explore.

"I thought he was never going to come out," Helena breathed to her mom, watching Caramel sniff the doors of the cupboards.

"I know. Why don't you put some food out for him?"

Helena stood up. She tried to do it very carefully and slowly, but Caramel still flinched back against the cupboards when he saw her move. It made her want to cry. "It's all right. I was just getting you some breakfast," she told him. "Lucy said she didn't feed you this morning, just in case you were sick in your basket."

She took one of the tins out of the cupboard and pulled up the ring on the lid. Then she laughed as Caramel hurried across the kitchen floor, his plastered leg knocking on the tiles. "You sound like a pirate cat with a wooden leg," she told him as she put the bowl down.

"I'm so glad he's eating," her mom said, leaning against the counter to watch him.

"I know—I was worried he'd be too upset being in a new place," Helena agreed. "But look at him. He's wolfing that down." She stood up, putting an arm around her mom. "Thanks for letting us have him."

"You're not disappointed?" Mom asked. "I mean, it's not like having a normal cat. He's not very friendly. And he can't sleep on your bed or anything like that."

Helena shrugged. "I know. But he will be able to one day. And I know he's not that friendly yet, but think how special it will be when he is."

She crouched down again to watch

Caramel licking his food bowl. He'd definitely gotten his appetite back, and he was making sure to get every last morsel of food. He stood up again, rather clumsily, and licked his whiskers.

Chapter Five
Settling In

Caramel uncurled himself from his basket as he heard footsteps coming toward the kitchen door. The girl. And probably breakfast. He hobbled to the door to meet her, rubbing hopefully around her ankles. She crouched down to pet him—but he noticed she carefully shut the kitchen door first, so he couldn't dart around it. She whispered to him as she scratched the satin-soft puffs of fur at the base of his ears, and he leaned against her lovingly.

Helena had spent a lot of the weekend sitting next to him on the floor, letting him get used to her being around. She'd even done her homework sitting on the kitchen floor. When Caramel had tried to steal her pencil while she was doing long division, it had been one of the best moments of the weekend. It proved he was happy enough to play.

"I wish I didn't have to go to school today...," Helena told him as she scooped food into his bowl. "Yuck. This smells disgusting, Caramel. I don't know how you can be so excited about it." She giggled, watching him waltz around her feet, waiting for her to put the bowl down. He still didn't like moving his broken leg much, so that leg stayed still, and the rest of him whirled around like a spinning top.

He started to gobble the food before she'd even put the bowl down, stretching up to get his mouth over the edge of the bowl, and batting at it with one golden paw.

"You're definitely getting better," Helena said, watching happily as he gulped the food down. "Are you making up for all those days at the vet's when you didn't eat properly? I do still wonder if you were a stray for a while before the accident. You're so thin. And I'm sure your owners would have seen our posters if they lived anywhere near. We put them everywhere."

Caramel was just finishing the food when Helena's mom hurried into the kitchen. She was a little late getting breakfast ready, and she was rushing. She banged the door open without thinking and Caramel shot into the corner, trembling and pressing himself against the side of the cupboard.

"Mom! You scared him!" Helena gasped.

"Oh! Sorry, Caramel...." Her mom shut the door gently and crouched down, holding her hand out for the frightened cat to sniff. "I'm really sorry, Helena, I didn't realize the door would frighten him so much. He's been so good this weekend."

"I know…," Helena agreed sadly. "But I suppose he's still upset, deep down. It's going to take a while for him to get over that." She looked at her mom. "He will be happier again one day, won't he?"

"I'm sure he will."

But Helena didn't think her mom was very sure at all.

"Be good, Caramel." Helena ran her hand lovingly down his silky back. "Get a lot of sleep. Grandma's going to come and see you at lunchtime, and I bet she'll bring you treats."

Caramel stood in the middle of the kitchen, looking up at her uncertainly. He wasn't sure what was happening. Since he had arrived at Helena's house early on Saturday morning, Helena had been with him almost all the time. She had even come down in the middle of the night to check on him. But now she had a coat on, and a bag with her. It looked as though she were leaving him behind.

At his old house, his owner had gone to work most days. Caramel had lazed the time away, curled up on the back of the couch so that he could watch the people passing in the street. And the cars. Caramel laid his ears back with a frightened little hiss.

Most days he'd slipped out his cat flap and patrolled his territory in the yards behind the house. There were several other cats in the street, and he was one of the youngest and newest, so he'd had to be careful to stay out of their way. But he still had plenty to explore. There was a pond a few houses away, and he liked to watch the frogs. And catch them sometimes. He could creep up on them among the plants around the water. But his owner hadn't liked it when Caramel had brought one home. He had taken Caramel's frog outside, then locked the cat flap so that he couldn't slip out and get it again.

But here, there was no window to watch from, and no cat flap to slip through. He was all alone in this little room. It was better than the cage at the animal hospital, of course, but being shut up still made him want to claw at the door and fight his way out. When would Helena and her mother come back? Maybe they weren't coming back at all. His old owner had fussed over him, and fed him, and loved him, but now he was gone. Maybe Helena was gone, too. Caramel stared anxiously at the kitchen door, hoping to hear them coming back. But there wasn't a sound.

Maybe he could go and find them himself....

Caramel hobbled across the tiled floor, sniffing hopefully at the door out to the yard. There was a faint breath of fresh air around the side of the door—just enough to make him desperate to go out. He scratched at the door, but not very hard. He could already see that he wasn't going to be able to get out.

Wearily, he trailed back to his basket. His broken back leg was aching, not used to carrying his weight. Caramel snuggled into the basket and hoped that Helena hadn't left him forever. He hoped that she would come back soon.

Chapter Six
A Great Idea

"So does anyone have any exciting news from the weekend?" Miss Smith looked around at the class as she finished taking attendance.

"Tell her!" Katie whispered, nudging Helena in the ribs with her elbow. "Helena does, Miss Smith!"

Helena turned pink, but she nodded. "I have a cat."

"Oh, wonderful!" Miss Smith smiled. "Where did you get him from, Helena? Or her?"

"He's a he. And he came from the animal hospital where my cousin Lucy works," Helena explained. "He was hit by a car last weekend."

Everyone in the class sat up and started listening more closely. Until then there'd been a bit of a Monday-ish feeling going on, and most people had been staring vaguely at the whiteboard, or whispering to each other.

"Hit by a car?" one of the boys asked. "What happened? Was he hurt?"

Helena nodded. "He has a broken back leg. But he was lucky. Usually they have to operate on cats and put pins in, but he just has a cast."

"But who does he belong to?" Miss Smith asked, sounding a little confused. "Was he a stray? Has no one claimed him?"

"No. And the animal hospital even put a little article about him in the local paper. That page where the rescue center usually puts a photo of a cat or dog who needs a home."

"Oh, that's how we got our dog!" Max called out. "We saw him in the paper."

"The article was in on Wednesday. But still no one claimed him. So we figured it was okay to take him home. We think maybe he's been lost for a while, even before he got hit by the car. He's really thin."

"Show them the photo," Katie suggested, and Helena pulled it out of her bag. She'd brought it in to show

Katie and a couple of her other friends. It was Caramel curled up asleep in his basket, and you could see his plaster cast. She passed it around, and all the class commented about how cute he was and how sad his leg looked.

"He came home with us because otherwise he would have had to go to the rescue center," Helena went on. "He's been really lucky. All his vet care has been paid for by donations from the rescue he almost went to. Vet bills can be really, really expensive. Hundreds of dollars, my cousin told me."

Helena frowned thoughtfully. Ever

since Molly, the vet, had told her that the rescue was helping to pay for Caramel's treatment, she'd been wishing she could do something to help. Something more than just giving them her allowance. She'd already decided to get her mom to buy their Christmas cards from the rescue—they made very cute ones with cats and dogs in the snow—but it would be good to think of a way to raise some money, too. So that if another cat got hurt like Caramel, it could be taken care of.

Lucy had said that when she'd called the rescue to tell them that they wouldn't have to take Caramel after all, the girl on the phone had been relieved. She'd said they were full. They needed a lot of money just to feed all the animals, let alone pay for vet care.

"Miss Smith, do you think we could try to raise some money for the rescue? Maybe we could have a bake sale or something," Helena asked hopefully. "Mr. Brown said he wanted all the classes to think about fundraising for charities. It was in assembly, back at the beginning of the school year."

"He did…," Miss Smith agreed. "It's a good idea. What about the rest of the class, though? What do you all think?"

"I definitely want to raise some money for the rescue!" Max nodded. "There were so many other dogs there when we went to get Chester. It was sad—my mom cried."

Everyone in the class was nodding, but Alice, another of Helena's friends, waved her hand at Miss Smith. "Can we do something different, though? Everyone does bake sales."

"That's because everyone likes cupcakes!" Katie pointed out, and Alice shrugged.

"It's still a little boring."

"So what do you want to do instead?" Miss Smith grinned. "How about a sponsored silence?"

Several people groaned, and Helena twisted her fingers in her hair, trying to think. They needed to come up with a good idea and quickly, before people lost interest. Already a couple of the boys were suggesting a sponsored parachute jump. It would just get silly in a minute. She put her hand up, looking hopefully at Miss Smith.

"We should do something that's about pets. That's what we're raising money for."

"Like a dog show!" Alice suggested, but Miss Smith shook her head.

"I'm sorry, Alice, but I don't think Mr. Brown would let us have a dog show in school," she said.

"But we could have a sort of competition," Helena said slowly. "With videos of our pets, instead of bringing the actual pets in! Like a funniest pet competition. We could ask the whole school if they wanted to enter. And the teachers! Mr. Brown has a really cute dog, doesn't he?"

"I could borrow my mom's phone and film Charlie skateboarding," Katie said excitedly. "He's not very good at it, but he loves trying. It's really funny to watch."

"And people could pay a little bit to enter," Helena said, still trying to think it through. "Then we could show all the videos at lunchtime. And sell tickets— oh, and have brownies and cookies for sale, too," she added to Katie.

"I'll ask Mr. Brown about it at lunchtime," Miss Smith said as the entire class tried to tell her about their pets' funniest tricks at once. "And then maybe we can use computer class this afternoon to make some posters."

Helena hopped impatiently from foot to foot as her mom unlocked the front door. Grandma had sent Mom a text saying that Caramel had been fine at lunchtime. But Helena was desperate to see for herself that he was all right. She rushed in as soon as Mom got the door open, heading for the kitchen.

"Oh! Listen!" she told her mom, stopping in the hall. "He's meowing. And I can hear him—he's gotten out of his basket, and he's coming to see us!" There was definitely a thumping noise coming from behind the kitchen door as Caramel limped determinedly toward them. Helena giggled. "Maybe I can film you doing your pirate walk for our competition," she told Caramel as she carefully opened the kitchen door. "Whoa! No running out...." She caught him gently. "Sorry, Caramel-cat. You have to stay in here."

Caramel half climbed into her lap, then rubbed his chin against her school sweater.

"Is he purring?" Mom whispered.

Helena looked up at her and nodded. She actually hadn't dared to say anything. It was only the second time she'd heard him purr. And that first time at the vet's he had only purred for a second or two, very faintly. Now Caramel was definitely purring. A deep, throaty purr that Helena could feel as well as hear.

"He's glad to see us," she whispered to Mom. "He's actually happy!"

Chapter Seven
Escape!

"He's definitely looking better," Katie said after school the next day, watching Caramel trying to investigate the fridge. Helena had opened it to get out the butter, and Caramel could smell the ham for her packed lunches. It smelled delicious—and very close to his nose.

"He is," Helena agreed happily. "No, you can't climb in there!" She nudged

Caramel back with her toe and closed the door. "Sorry, Caramel."

Caramel stalked away with his tail in the air as though he wasn't bothered, but his plastered leg made it a little tricky. He was still feeling wobbly.

"He looked sad in that photo you brought in," Katie said. "But now he's cheered up a lot, I think. It's great to finally meet him in person. Caramel! Here, kitty…." Caramel padded cautiously across the floor toward her, sniffing her outstretched fingers and letting her rub his head and tickle his ears.

"He's much more friendly now," Helena said happily. "I don't think he'd have done that on Saturday when we brought him home. And it's only Wednesday. He's gotten so much better, and in such a short time. When he was still at the vet's, he was so shy and miserable. He's still nervous sometimes, though," she added. "He hates loud noises."

"He walks really well, doesn't he?" Katie said, watching Caramel prowl around their ankles as they measured the ingredients for their cookies.

"He's putting weight on his bad leg a little more now. Before he was sort of hopping, as if he was trying not to put it down onto the ground. He's got another two and a half weeks, and then hopefully he can have the cast taken off. Can you please pass me the sugar?"

The girls were making cat-shaped cookies to sell at the Funniest Pet Show. Mr. Brown, the principal, had said it was a great idea, very creative. He'd told them to go ahead and arrange the show for Friday, when he'd be able to judge.

"Did you send in a video of Caramel with his cast on?" Katie asked. "I filmed Charlie. He was great! The skateboard went out from under his paws and he just sort of stared at it as if he didn't understand what had happened."

"Yes, I sent it, but I don't think he'll win," Helena said, shaking her head. "Some of the others are so funny. Bella's cat trying to drink out of the faucet in the bathroom is the best. It's the way she turns her head upside down, and then shakes all the water off her whiskers. It makes me laugh every time."

Helena and some of her classmates had been watching the videos with their teacher during recess and lunch to find the best ones to go in the show. They'd wanted to put them all in, but there were so many. They had already made more than $80, just from people paying a dollar to send in a video. They also were selling tickets for the show, and everyone in the class was supposed to be bringing some brownies or cookies to sell, too.

"We should have gotten gold frosting for the eyes on these cookies," Katie said, peering down at Caramel, who'd gone to sit in his basket under the counter, since they clearly weren't going to feed him anything. "I hadn't noticed before what a beautiful color his eyes are."

"I know," Helena agreed proudly. "Mom and I talked about doing the eyes gold when we made the shopping list, but we decided green ones were more common. Caramel's just extra-specially beautiful."

"He looks like he's sulking," Katie said. "Is he okay? He has his nose tucked down inside his basket."

Helena looked down under the counter and sighed. "I think now that he's walking better, it's making him upset being shut in the kitchen. Every time we open the kitchen door, he's there, trying to slip around our legs. He never scratches or bites, but you can tell he's annoyed. His ears go all flat, and his tail twitches. He wants to go and explore."

"Couldn't you let him out?" Katie asked. "Why does he have to stay in the kitchen?"

"Molly—that's the vet—said that if he tried to climb or jump, he could jar his broken leg and hurt it again. Even if he were just trying to climb the stairs, he might trip and fall because of the cast. There's nowhere in the kitchen that he can reach to jump up to, but there's enough space for him to exercise his leg muscles. Otherwise his leg's going to be thin and weak inside the cast."

Katie nodded. "That makes sense."

"Caramel doesn't think so, though. He thinks we're just being mean." Helena sighed. "Little grumpy-face," she told Caramel lovingly.

Caramel heard her and looked up. He gazed at her for a moment and then yawned hugely, showing all his teeth and his bright pink tongue.

Helena giggled. "See? That's what he thinks of us."

Caramel sat by the back door, his nose pressed against the narrow crack between the door and the frame. There was something out in the yard, he was sure. He could hear it—a bird, maybe, tapping and twittering around on the little stone patio. He wanted to be out there, too, smelling the smells, chasing the birds.

357

Just feeling the air ruffling up his fur. He hated being an indoor cat.

He paced up and down beside the door for a few moments, letting out a frustrated meow. His leg was so much better now. It felt stronger. He was sure he could even climb a tree, if only they would let him out. Or maybe scramble up onto the top of a fence, just to get a good look around. He wanted to see what the outside was like around here. He was so sick of being stuck indoors.

His ears twitched as he caught a sound from the front of the house— footsteps on the path, and now scratching as someone fiddled with the front door. Helena was back!

No. His shoulders sagged a little.

It wasn't the right time. It would be that other lady who comes to check on him.

"Hello, Caramel...." Grandma squeezed carefully around the door, making sure not to let him get out. "How are you, sweetie? Want a treat?" She brought a packet out of her purse, and Caramel sniffed as she pulled it open. The delicious smell wafted around. But somehow, it just wasn't very exciting. Not nearly as good as the fresh-air smell through the back door. It was starting to rain now. He could smell the wet pavement smell and hear the heavy, fat drops pattering down on the stone. He wanted to be out in it. Not for long—just enough to feel the freshness, and then dash back in and lick off all the water. It would be so good....

"Oh, it's raining! And I didn't bring an umbrella." Grandma was staring out of the window, looking irritated. "And look, Caramel, they have the laundry outside! Well, that's going to get soaked. And there's Helena's school sweater. I wonder if she needs that for tomorrow.... I'll have to go and bring it all in."

She put down her bag on the

counter and hurried to the door, jingling the keys as she unlocked it.

Caramel hadn't understood what she was saying about the laundry, of course, but he knew what the sound of the keys meant. She was letting him out! He stood by her feet, his tail twitching excitedly, and his whiskers fanned and bristling. Out! After all this time! As the door opened, he darted around Grandma's feet, his caramel fur brushing against her legs, and hopped down the little step onto the patio.

Grandma was thinking about the laundry, not about Caramel, so she didn't realize what had happened until it was too late. "Oh! Oh, no! You're not supposed to go out! Oh, my goodness...." She left the laundry and went after the cat. "Caramel! Come on … Caramel … Kitty, kitty…."

But Caramel was sniffing at the flowerpots and twitching delightedly at the feel of the rain on his fur. He could smell other cats, which was interesting, and dangerous, and exciting. And perhaps a dog, close by, and there was a beetle walking along in front of his nose. Everything was good.

"Come here, Caramel, come on, you'll hurt yourself…." Grandma reached down and tried to grab him, but Caramel skittered out of reach, his cast knocking on the stone paving, and throwing him off balance.

He hissed as a twinge of pain ran through his injured leg, and backed away furiously.

"Oh, no...." Grandma hurried after him, but Caramel hissed again, frightened and hurting, and darted away around the corner of the house, up the little side alley where the garbage cans were.

Grandma was chasing him, but he didn't want to be caught. His leg was throbbing as he scurried up the alley, and now there was a gate, shutting him in again. Caramel spat angrily and pressed up against it. He wasn't going to let her grab him! He couldn't be shut up inside again. He thrust a clawed paw at Grandma as she came close and reached to pick him up. Desperate, he squashed himself down and scrambled under the wooden gate, dragging his plastered leg behind him. He struggled, meowing, for a second— and then he was out, at the front of the house, on the road.

Once he'd squeezed under the gate, Caramel hobbled out onto the pavement, going as fast as he could with his plastered leg. He was determined not to let Grandma catch him. He scurried along the pavement and darted behind someone's garbage can when he heard the gate squeak open, and Grandma dash out after him. He could hear her calling, but he stayed tucked behind the can.

Caramel peered out, watching her, and when she hurried off the other way down the road, he pressed himself close against the wall and slunk away. Everything smelled so good in the damp, rain-fresh air. His leg was aching a little—he hadn't gone so fast or so far on it in a long time—but he didn't mind. He was tired of cages and that tiny room.

The rain had stopped now, and the clouds were blowing over. He shivered with pleasure as he felt the warm autumn sun shining down on his fur. That was what he wanted to do! He would find somewhere to lie in the sun. If only Grandma hadn't been chasing him, he could have stayed in the little yard in the back of Helena's house. He was sure there would have been a nice sunny place to curl up. And when Helena came home, she could pet him while he snoozed.

He glanced uncertainly back down the road. He could go and see. He could squeeze back under the gate…. But he could hear Grandma calling him, her voice more and more worried. That high, panicked note made the fur lift a little along his spine, and he hurried on a few steps farther.

He couldn't go too far, though, he realized, after he'd gone past a few more houses. It was hard, half hopping along with his cast like this, and he was already getting tired.

He was looking around, wondering where he could go and sleep in the sun for a little while, when he heard it. It drowned out Grandma's shouting— the low rumble of a car, heading down the road toward him.

Caramel's ears went back, and his tail fluffed out to twice its normal size. He had heard cars before, of course. But now the sound reminded him of the accident, and that strange blaze of light, and then waking up to find he couldn't walk.

He whipped his head desperately from side to side as the growl of the car grew louder, and as it roared past he shot into the nearest yard, forgetting how much his leg was hurting, and how tired he was. He had to get away.

Caramel darted under the bushes, not even noticing how wet they were. And then he huddled there, shivering and terrified, and wishing he'd never strayed outside the house.

Chapter Eight
Home Again

"He got out?" Helena gaped at Grandma as they stood outside the gates after school. She couldn't understand it. For a moment when Grandma had started to explain, Helena had thought that she must be joking—that it was some sort of silly story, but it wasn't.

"I'm so sorry, Helena. I wasn't thinking. It was the laundry, you see—

I had to bring it in because of the rain. Oh, I'm not explaining this very well."

Grandma looked exhausted, Helena realized. She'd probably spent a long time trying to get Caramel back in the house. She felt guilty for being angry, but only a little bit. How could Grandma have let him out, when it was so important that he stayed in the kitchen?

"He slipped past me. He was so quick...."

"We might need to get him to the vet's to see if he's hurt his leg." Helena started off down the road toward home, weaving around everyone pouring out of the school gates. Usually they went back to Grandma's house on the days that Mom was working late, but Helena was sure Grandma would understand that she wanted to check on Caramel first.

"How did you get him back in?" she asked, turning to look at Grandma, who was hurrying after her.

Grandma stopped and simply stared at her, and Helena's stomach seemed to lurch inside her. All at once, she knew what Grandma had been trying to make her understand.

She hadn't gotten him back inside. Caramel was lost!

Helena turned back, looking at the road and the cars flashing by, taking everyone home from school. Then she simply ran. She ran all the way home, ignoring Grandma calling after her. After a little while, she couldn't hear Grandma shouting anyway.

Her mouth was dry, her heart racing.

She was so horribly certain that as she turned into their street, she would see the little heap of sandy fur again. And that this time, Caramel wouldn't have been so lucky. He had his leg in a cast—how could he get out of the way of a car?

When she turned the corner onto their road, Helena stopped for a moment, panting, her face scarlet. There was no cat in the road, not that she could see. And no crowd of horrified passers-by. She took a deep, shuddering breath and went on, hurrying up their side of the road, and then carefully crossing over and checking the other side, looking under all the cars.

At last she stopped, leaning against the front wall of their house and trying not to cry. Where was he? Grandma had tried to explain that he'd run under the side gate, so he must have come out onto the road. *Maybe he's just hiding somewhere,* Helena thought, with a sudden jolt of hope. She dropped her school bag by the front door and set off up the road, calling, "Caramel! Caramel!"

But he didn't come, and she couldn't even hear an answering meow. She flinched as a car sped past, wanting to shout after the driver to slow down. What if Caramel ran across the road to get to her?

Would he come anyway? Helena wondered worriedly. Maybe he didn't know her well enough to want to come back. He'd only lived with them for half a week. But he'd been getting so friendly— she had really felt like he was their cat.

Maybe he'd gone back to his old house—his old owner—if he knew where it was. Helena gulped back tears.

"Helena!" Grandma was hurrying down the road toward her. "Oh, I was so worried. You crossed all those roads on your own."

Helena stared back at her. "I'm sorry, Grandma," she said breathlessly. She'd been so frightened, she'd just thought about getting home and finding Caramel, nothing else.

"He's not here, Grandma," Helena said miserably. "I've called and called. Maybe he's gone back to his old home. Or he might just be lost. He might be one of those cats who doesn't have a good sense of direction. He'll never find his way back to us!"

Grandma wrapped her arms around Helena. "We'll find him," she told her. "I'm so sorry, Helena. Surely he can't be far away."

Caramel could hear Helena calling him, and his ears pricked forward hopefully. She sounded worried, but he knew her much better than Grandma, and he was sure she wasn't angry. He stirred under the bushes, trying to gather the energy to get back onto his aching leg and go to her. But as he poked his nose out from under the plants, another car came racing by, and he pressed himself back into the leaves with a frightened hiss.

He couldn't move. He just couldn't.

Even though he could hear Helena calling him again and again, and her grandma and later her mom, too, he was too frightened to come out. Every few minutes a car would go by, and Caramel froze, paralyzed by the noise.

He wriggled back even farther when a car pulled up outside the house and footsteps echoed beside his hiding place. It was getting dark, and cold. The cold made his injured leg ache even more, and he shivered miserably. The lights came on in the house behind him, and that just made the night seem darker. He wanted to be home, with Helena putting down his food bowl, and watching him eat.

There were fewer cars now, though, he realized. He had been hiding there for hours, waiting for the next one to roar past, his muscles tensed in case it came close. He edged out from the bushes, his whiskers twitching nervously as he sniffed the night air. Helena's house was only a little way down the road. He knew it.

He could get home, if only he were brave enough to come out of his hiding place.

And it was home, he realized. He wanted to be back with Helena. Even if they did keep him closed up in that room. The house was safe and warm, and they would take care of him. Caramel limped out of the tiny front yard and crouched by the wall, his ears laid back. No cars. It was time to go.

Helena was sitting curled up in bed, in the dark. She'd tried to sleep—Mom kept coming in and checking on her, and the last time Helena had actually pretended she was asleep. She didn't want Mom to tell her again that it would be all right, and they'd probably find Caramel tomorrow. Mom didn't know that! She was just saying it to make her feel better. And it wasn't working.

Helena sniffed. She had tried so hard to take care of Caramel, but it would have been better if he'd gone to the rescue after all. He wouldn't have been able to run away there, and he'd still be safe. She felt a choking feeling build up in her throat again, and she tried desperately to swallow it back down.

What if they never saw him again?

Helena gulped and buried her nose in her comforter, trying to muffle the gasping, horrible noises she was making. It was really late—Mom was probably asleep. She sat there, curled up and shaking, tears making a wet patch on her comforter.

He hadn't been hit by another car, Helena tried to tell herself. They had searched all the streets nearby, and they hadn't found him. And Grandma had called Lucy to check that he hadn't been brought into the animal hospital. He was just hiding somewhere. She pressed her face back into the comforter, thinking how cold and frightened Caramel must be. The wind lashed raindrops against her window again—it was such an awful night to be outside.

Then another sound made Helena look up. She could hardly hear it, with the wind blowing, and at first she'd thought it was just the rain. But it wasn't—she knew that noise! That odd knocking, like a pirate walking on his wooden leg. Helena wriggled frantically, trying to unwind herself from her comforter. It was Caramel!

She jumped out of bed, racing to the

window. She could hear him meowing now, too. She threw open her curtains and shoved the window open, leaning down to see into the yard.

And he was there! A small, bedraggled, golden cat, yowling at her in the moonlight. He'd come home!

"Look, Caramel," Helena told him proudly as she stuck the certificate on to the fridge door with a magnet. "Bella's cat won the prize for the most amazing pet! I told you she would, but you were second! And do you know how much money we raised altogether? Three hundred dollars! That's a lot," she added, as Caramel rubbed himself around her knees. "Yes, I know. You don't care at all. You just want me to get the cat food out. All right."

She looked down at him as she scooped the food into his bowl. His fur was soft and silky again, and he was only limping a little. Last night, when she'd run downstairs and out into the yard to scoop him up, his coat had been dark and spiky with rain, and he'd looked so miserable. His leg had obviously been hurting, too. She and Mom had dried him with a towel, and he'd purred gratefully. Helena had been worried that the rain had softened the cast, or that he'd made the break worse, but Molly had come over and looked at him, and said that it was all right. She thought Caramel was just limping because he'd been putting more weight on his leg than he was used to.

"Only another two weeks," Helena told Caramel as she knelt on the floor, watching him licking the food out of his bowl. "Molly said she was almost sure the cast could come off after that. Then you'll be able to explore the rest of the house. And go outside."

Caramel sniffed around the edge of the

bowl in case any food had escaped, and then nosed lovingly at Helena's hand. He yawned and licked his whiskers, then climbed into her lap. He flopped down, stretching his plastered leg sideways, and kneaded at her school skirt with his front paws. He was glad to be home.

Helena giggled and shifted her feet a little so she wouldn't get pins and needles. It looked like Caramel was staying for a while.